POWER OF THE GODDESS

GRECIAN GODDESS TRILOGY: BOOK 2

TESSA COLE
CLARA WILS

Gryphon's Gate Publishing

Power of the Goddess

Gryphon's Gate Publishing

550 King St. N.

PO Box 42088 Conestoga

Waterloo, ON

N2L 6K5

ebook ISBN: 978-1-988115-92-4

Print ISBN: 978-1-988115-91-7

CHAPTER 1

ANNIE

HALF A DOZEN, BIG, TOUGH, NO-NONSENSE SECURITY MEN from the convention center looked at me, although none of them were as big or tough as the two guys, Keph and Rion, who flanked me.

We stood in the middle of a large room with a stage that had a long table on it, waiting for a panel to present at the comic convention. Half of the chairs had been set out for the audience, and half of those chairs had been crushed or tossed aside. And there was no way the security guards hadn't noticed.

Except I couldn't let that distract them. The *naiad* had infected who-knew-how-many people at this convention, and I couldn't let anyone leave without figuring out how to heal them with magical powers that I shouldn't have in my world and yet still did. That, and I wouldn't be able to do that if the security men took me into custody.

Which meant I had to take control of this situation.

The trouble was. I wasn't that sort of woman. I was

quiet and reserved. I didn't face things head on. There was a reason I wanted to live alone in some tropical paradise.

But I'd gotten myself into this mess. I'd chosen to chase after the *naiad* and Disease Man and try to save as many people as I could, and I needed to do something about it now.

I just had to figure out what powerful Annie Chambers looked like.

"Listen up!" I shouted, just a little too loud. The men before me started and from the side of my vision I caught Rion twitch as well. "We have an emergency situation here, and I'm going to need all of your help with this."

The security guards stared at me with a mix of surprise, confusion, and disbelief.

Swell.

"That woman my men just apprehended is a bio-terrorist," I said before they could question me. "She's been releasing a nasty disease on the premises. I've stopped her, but there's no clue how many people she's infected. I need a level three quarantine set up on this facility, all exits closed, and everyone ready for my inspection."

"Who are you?" one of the men managed to say. He stepped forward, perhaps a leader, not the largest of the men, but seeming less confused than the others.

"Annie Chambers." That much was true.

And now time for some confident lies.

"Special Agent in Charge of the FBI's Bio-Terrorism team. These are my men—" I hadn't shown ID and the man who'd spoken up frowned with skepticism. I turned to Rion. "This is Ryan—" I needed a last name quick, and seeing him shirtless reminded me of our time in bed which made my lips quirk in a smile that I hoped no one saw and a single word jump to mind.

Jeez I had a dirty mind.

"Long," I said. "Agent Ryan Long." I turned to Keph. "This is—" Keph...? No. His name, like Rion's, was too weird and would draw suspicion. "Kevin." My mind jumped to Keph's *member* and my dirty mind couldn't stop coming up with descriptive names for them. If Rion was long, then Keph was... "Thicke."

"Can I see some ID?"

"There's no time for this," I said, pushing on as if I hadn't heard him and praying he'd give up and get to saving people. "People are infected out there and the longer you stand here, the worse things are going to get."

I stalked up to the lead security guy. He was half a foot taller than me, but I met him gaze-for-gaze, eyes hard, with all the certainty and urgency I could muster.

He took a step back.

Ha! Yeah!

Oh... Wait.

That was probably because Keph had just stepped up close behind me.

"Move! Now!" I shouted.

At the same time Keph growled, "You heard her."

"Yes, ma'am." The security man turned to the others. "You heard her, go."

They hurried from the room and the guy in charge took two big steps away from me—or rather away from

Keph—and shot me a dark look. "I'm calling the FBI, though. Confirming your story."

"Good," I said with a spark of fire in my voice. "And while you're at it, call the police. Your men will probably need help here to keep this contained."

He huffed, but thankfully didn't put up more of a fight and rushed out of the room.

Once he was out of earshot all the bluster drained out of me. "Holy-fucking-wow! I can't believe that worked!" A cold sweat trickled down the insides of my arms and another pool was forming between my breasts.

Fuck, that had been too close. I was sure the only reason those men had listened to me was because I'd had Keph backing me up. Speaking of which...

I turned to the guys.

"Thanks," I said, blowing out a huff of air, my body starting to tremble with the shock of fighting and capturing the *naiad* and then lying to the security guard. But I couldn't lose it now. There were people here who needed healing, far too many people, possibly thousands of them. This was going to be a long day.

"I'm exhausted, but we need to heal as many people here as possible."

"Those men are corralling everyone. There'll be time to heal them, though I fear what that will do to you," Rion said as he put his jacket back on, the dark material accentuating his bronzed skin, pale blond hair, and blue eyes. God he was sexy and the open jacket instantly drew my eyes to his naked, chiseled chest and hard abs.

I wanted to rip that jacket right off and—

No not the jacket. He could leave that on while his

pants came off and he pushed that incredible cock of his into me once again. I shuddered, growing hot, and the look in his eyes grew just as hungry as I felt.

Suddenly I had lots of energy.

I laughed, was sex the answer? After the last time with him, I'd been a pool of jelly with no strength at all. So, perhaps not.

But the intensity of my desire swelled. There was no way I'd be able to concentrate without relieving the pressure.

And if I kept it to a tease, maybe that would give me the energy or in the least the motivation to push through and wrap this mess up quickly.

That, and Rion was right. It would take a moment or two for those guys to lock down this place and I wasn't going to be able to stand there and wait. Not while I was suddenly aware of Rion and how I knew—because of amazing firsthand experience—how he could make me feel.

Then my gaze flicked to Keph.

The heat in my chest sunk deeper, my breath catching as the flash of the three of us together came to mind. Keph with his huge... well... everything.

Oh, yes, please!

I grabbed their hands and began leading them to the doors at the other end of the room, in the opposite direction the security guards had gone. "I have a plan to get me some more energy." Not to mention get me thinking straight, because now having sex— No, just a tease. Having a tease was all I could think about, even though I *knew* I should be thinking about the mess at hand. "And it involves the both of you."

"Whatever you need," Keph said softly, his deep voice rumbling through me, bringing a smile to my face. I'd hoped he'd say something like that.

"Annie, what's this plan?" Rion asked, his tone more hesitant than Keph's.

"We need to find some place to be alone. Then you two are going to get me all worked up so I have the energy to heal ten thousand people."

"I, ah..." Rion frowned, looking pained, clearly wanting to say yes but questioning the efficacy of the plan. "I can't say I'm not... intrigued, but are you certain that will give you energy and not take it from you?"

"As long as I don't get off, then sure... I think so." I shrugged off my doubt. "Either way, I'll feel a whole lot better." Or so I hoped. I couldn't see how I'd feel bad after sex with these two. Sore maybe, but not bad. And this wasn't sex. This was just a really good tease to get me all worked up and get me motivated. That was all.

The trick would be stopping there.

There were two sets of doors at the back of the room that led to a hall, the direction Del and Aethan had gone with the naiad, and another single door next to it, leading to a storage room. It was probably going to be the most private place I could find. It was dark inside and there wasn't anyone there. A large, floor to ceiling metal shelf ran along the right wall close to the door filled with cleaning supplies, toilet paper, paper towels, linens, and other stuff, while stacks of tables and chairs filled the rest of the room. I flicked the light on and looked around. No other entrances.

Even better.

I pulled the guys inside. "Keph, close that door and keep your back to it, so we're not interrupted," I ordered. My body thrummed with need, and I was suddenly jittery, excited, and apparently back in command mode.

Keph did as I'd asked, leaning his massive back against the door, and my pulse leaped into a quick tattoo.

Oh, God.

This was really going to happen.

Was I crazy?

Probably. But I knew I'd be even more crazy trying to concentrate past my sudden, aching desire. I wouldn't be able to fight it along with my exhaustion and worry, so I might as well get my desire out of the way.

"How would you like us to... work you up?" Rion asked.

I glanced at him then Keph. The three of us were standing there, awkward. This was all a bit staged... but screw it.

This was definitely what I wanted and I wasn't going to get anywhere with my clothes on so I pulled off my jacket and shoved it onto the rack beside me. I reached to pull off my sweater but Rion stepped close and captured my wrists in his hands.

"Let me," he murmured, his smooth tenor sending a shiver rushing down my spine.

I lifted my gaze to meet his. His pupils were dilated with desire, turning his blue eyes into bottomless dark blue depths that made my pulse pound.

"Okay," I breathed and he slid his hands to my shoulders and turned me away from him to face Keph.

A moment of disappointment flashed through me at the loss of eye contact, but he pressed his hard body against my back, and I could feel his erection, large and hard against my rear through my thick skirt.

Oh, yes. That was what I wanted—

No.

Not what I wanted... at least not right now.

The plan was for just a tease, to get worked up enough and be motivated enough to heal everyone here and *then* come back for more.

He grabbed the bottom of my sweater and slowly lifted it, the action so simple and yet, so damn sexy.

I raised my arms and he drew the sweater off and set it on the shelf beside my coat then slid his hands back down my arms, skimming the edge of my breasts sending a thrill rushing through me despite the fact that I was still wearing a T-shirt and bra.

My pulse roared in my ears and my breath picked up. Was it me or was the storeroom getting really hot, really quickly?

Maybe asking for just a tease was a bad idea.

But even as I thought that, I locked gazes with Keph, who watched Rion slowly undress me.

Desire filled his silver-rimmed black eyes, and while I wasn't sure I'd be able to tell if he was flushed given his glistening onyx skin, just that look in his eyes and seeing the hungry, aching need there was more than enough to tell he was aroused. And that made something in my chest swell. It was a matching need, except it felt deeper than just a desire for physical release. It was like I craved a connection with him, which was crazy because I didn't know Keph or any of the guys well enough to crave a deep connection with them. *Want* maybe, but not *crave*. Not yet.

Rion grabbed the hem of my long-sleeved T-shirt, leaned close, and brushed his lips against the sensitive skin behind my ear.

A soft moan escaped my lips and I tilted my head to the side to give him better access, but didn't take my gaze off Keph. The big man's chest rose and fell, his breath getting faster too, each inhalation expanding his bulky muscles and straining his white dress shirt. The sleeves had been too tight so he'd ripped those off and now all I could think about was ripping off the rest of it.

God! This was taking forever.

But then... it was supposed to be a tease wasn't it?

The muscles in Keph's jaw tightened and the big man fumbled with the tiny-to-him zipper on his pants, trying to free his erection. The fabric bulged, reminding me of just how large he was. I'd seen him and the others naked since clothing was optional in their world and had dreamed about what it would be like to have sex with him.

Oh yes, break that beast out.

Rion's breath came faster as well now, his desire clearly rising like mine and Keph's. He pulled off my T-shirt, his pace, like his breath, no longer slow, as if he was losing control as well.

Keph finally found the zipper and pulled it down, but hadn't undone the button, and wasn't free.

He grunted, as Rion undid the clasp on my bra and let the lacy fabric fall away, then Keph gasped as if the sight of my breasts had stollen his breath.

Heat pooled between my thighs and my core ached. I was so very ready for one of these men to be inside me— Well I was ready for Rion. I wasn't so sure about Keph yet, but I had no doubt with a little more attention from them, I would be.

Except this was just supposed to be a tease.

If I was smart. I'd stop things where we were. I was certainly full of energy for *something* right now, and that something was supposed to be healing everyone in the convention center. But I couldn't bring myself to say it. I wanted more. I wanted to feel Rion's hands on my skin, wanted to see how large and dark Keph's eyes would get with his need.

The large man finally succeeded in popping the button at the top of his pants without ripping it off and freed his monster erection, breathing a heavy sigh of relief.

Rion's hands found my breasts, clutching them greedily, and I gasped at the hard grip, a sudden contrast to the slow, soft, and sensual touch he'd used to undress me. He sucked on the skin behind my ear and kneaded my girls, tightening my nipples into stiff, aching buds with an onslaught of passionate sensation.

My legs grew weak and I leaned back into him. My breath was ragged and I moaned my pleasure, my body throbbing with need.

"Too much?" Rion asked, his lips against my skin, his hands still working my breasts.

Oh, hell yes. We were beyond teasing now, and it was exactly what I wanted.

"No," I gasped.

And that was it. I'd fully committed. To hell with this being just a tease. I'd lose my mind if he stopped now.

CHAPTER 2

KEPHAS

I'D NEVER BEEN THIS AROUSED IN MY LIFE.

Oh, I'd been aroused and been with women a few times. Oddly, I'd never been with another stone titan. Being a secluded and private people, mating was saved for after the bonding ceremony. But in my adventures to Masia to see my fellow emissaries, I'd had a few women.

Few.

There hadn't been many who'd wanted to be with me after seeing my full size, but a brave few had tried, while even fewer had succeeded.

They'd required a lot of 'working up' as Annie seemed to call it, before they were ready for me. They'd ride me, carefully, and leave happy, but I'd never truly been able to fully be with a woman. None would be able to take the full force of my thrusts, and Annie probably wouldn't be able to either

Except right now, watching Rion strip and fondle her, I was so ready to try.

I wouldn't, not without her say-so, which I was certain

she wouldn't give, not now, since she'd made it clear she only wished to be aroused. But I couldn't help being turned on and the pain in my cock as it strained against my pants, had been so intense, I feared I'd have ripped the fragile fabric if I hadn't released it.

Except now that it was free, it was so much harder to remember I couldn't go any further.

It took everything I had to just stay put, keep my hands to myself, and let Annie see how amazingly sexy I found her without touching her. Her intense gaze never left me, moving from my eyes to my cock and back again, and she licked her lips, making my pulse stutter in an anticipation I shouldn't have.

Soft moans escaped her lips and she moved against Rion as if she was fully aroused even though she'd assured him that what he was doing wasn't too much yet.

Rion's hands left her gorgeous, full breasts, sliding down to her hips and drew her back hard. She tensed with a gasp, her eyes starting to roll back, her long eyelashes fluttering.

This certainly seemed like too much. It was almost too much for me and from the dark need in Rion's eyes, it was almost too much for him, too.

I waited for her command to stop, but it didn't come.

Apparently, it took a lot to tease our little goddess.

Rion slid his thumbs under the waistband of her skirt and ran his hands to her back where her garment was secured, his next action clear: remove the rest of her clothes.

"Are you sure you want more?" he whispered.

She nodded as if she couldn't find her voice, and he

knelt and pushed her skirt, skin-tight pants—she'd called them leggings—and her underthings down her legs. My breath stalled, watching her flesh being revealed.

He helped her step out of her boots and the clothes, one foot, then the other, which left her standing beautiful and naked before me.

It took all my willpower to keep from coming at the sight of her. She was unlike any woman I'd ever seen before and I'd been mesmerized from the moment I'd seen her. Her pale fiery hair, her full round hips and ample bust and those odd, but somehow enticing, spots all over her face, arms, and chest. Gods above she was stunning.

"It's your turn Keph," Rion said, and as he rose, he put one hand behind each of her thighs, and lifted her from her feet.

"Oh, yes," she breathed, as he stepped closer to me and opened her legs in invitation.

"Are you sure?" I glanced from her to Rion and back again. Her gaze was simmering with desire... and so was Rion's. "You two are bonded."

"Bonds aren't the same in this world," Rion said. "Even if they were, this doesn't feel wrong, and if I hadn't been a fool that night, I would have realized that." He teased his lips along her jaw, drawing her gaze to him. "I don't know if it's because you're from a different world or if you really are a goddess, but I know you'll never be mine alone and I'm fine with that. I want you to have anything and everything that makes you happy. Keph," he turned his attention back to me. "It's your turn... if that's what the goddess wishes."

She half huffed half moaned as if a mix of emotions had swept through her. "I'm not a goddess."

"You are to me," he replied. "And is it?"

She frowned at him. "Is it what?"

"Is it your wish for Keph to work you up, too?"

"Oh, yes." Her gaze jumped to me, her eyes filled with sexual hunger, making my cock throbbed even more.

Except I couldn't give her that, not without breaking the rules that we should just tease her. Also she'd need more 'working up' for her to be ready for me.

Instead, I sank to my knees, making sure one foot was still on the door behind me to keep it closed, and ran my hands along the inside of her thighs.

Her breath hitched the closer I got to her folds, and left her altogether on a low, sensual groan, when I teased my thumb along her opening, feeling her wetness and desire for us.

"Oh, yes," she said again, and I gently probed her opening, slowly sliding in one finger.

It filled her, not completely, but close. I began a slow rhythmic stroke of that tender flesh and leaned closer, teasing my lips over the top of her left thigh and inching closer to where my finger filled her.

She moaned her pleasure and captured my cheeks between her tiny, delicate hands, figuring out what I intended with my lips. Except instead of pushing me away, she urged me closer, giving me permission.

Rion lifted her slightly to meet my lips, and I swept my tongue from my finger up to the hardened sensitive nub that I knew drew the most amazing sounds from women.

Annie was no exception. She gasped, her body tensing, her eyes rolling back with pleasure before she released a low sensual moan.

My cock ached, desperate for a release, but I kept my gaze locked on hers, waiting for the moment when she said stop.

Except I was starting to get the impression she wasn't going to say the word, and a part of me really liked the idea that she desired Rion and I so much she couldn't help herself.

I slid my finger in deeper, in and out, in and out, as I kissed and sucked around it, always coming back to the sensitive nub.

Her breath turned ragged and little whimpers and gasping moans fell from her lips.

"This is too much," Rion groaned, his breath just as fast, his body trembling, but not with the effort to hold her. She was so small I had no doubt he could hold her for hours. Which meant he had to be fighting his own need.

"No," she begged. "More."

"Any more and you'll come," Rion said.

"I don't care." She squirmed against him, her hips rocking forward—as much as they could in his grip—to meet my finger and mouth. "This is what I want."

And she did.

It hadn't struck me right away, but I could see now that she was glowing. Her skin gave off a faint luminescence similar to Rion's glow when he'd first made love to her, similar to the light emanating from his face now.

"You're both glowing," I said, stopping my work

between Annie's legs for a moment. This seemed significant.

Annie glanced down at herself. "Holy fuck."

Rion moved her away from me and gently set her on her feet, but she trembled and clung to him as if her legs wouldn't hold her, and he held her tight to help her stay standing.

"What is this?" Annie asked.

I didn't know, but it made her look even more amazing, certainly more like the goddess we'd all thought her to be initially. Perhaps...?

"Can't you feel it?" Rion said softly. "Our bond."

She looked him in his sky-blue eyes and then her own golden eyes widened. "I... do."

"What are you feeling?" I asked, as I stood. It seemed the pleasuring was done for now.

"I felt a connection when we bonded," Rion said. "Something... magical that was truly tying us together. That kiss we shared was far more powerful than just a bond kiss. There was magic to it in this world or..." He looked at Annie. "Or in you."

"In me?" Annie's eyes widened even more. "No. I'm not spe—" Her expression turned sad and I didn't have to wonder what she was thinking. It had been obvious in how embarrassed she'd been when it had come out that she wasn't really a goddess.

"Special?" I finished for her. She looked at me, those gold eyes literally shining, and nodded. "But you can heal in your world," I continued. Another nod. That's what she'd been pondering as well that had made her reconsider her words.

"So?" I prompted.

"Perhaps I am...?" She couldn't finish and it broke my heart.

"You *are* special. Even if you didn't have magic in your world, you'd still be special," Rion said, his voice filled with devotion and love. "You're magical."

She tangled her fingers in his hair and drew her lips to his in a long, deep, impassioned kiss. Both of their bodies began to glow brighter. It was going to be blinding in here soon.

She broke off from him, breathing hard, her gaze locked on her glowing arm.

"I'm magical," she whispered, then a stunned, giddy expression flooded her face. "I'm magical!"

In the next moment, her expression changed to a wide-eyed realization of some sort. Then she slowly turned to me. "And I know exactly how to get the strength I need to heal thousands of people."

I was confused. She was looking at me so intently

She stepped away from Rion, her legs steadier now, and reached out to me. "Keph, get those lips down here, so I can kiss you."

My heart skipped a beat, my own realization flooding me. She wanted to bond with me.

CHAPTER 3

ANNIE

KEPH'S EYES WENT WIDE AS HE KNELT AGAIN. REMEMBERING why he'd knelt the first time made my knees wobble even more. He was certainly a master with his fingers and lips—

His lips, yes, back to the task at hand.

I didn't really know how the fuck I was magical, but I couldn't deny it was happening. Apparently sex with Rion— no *kissing* Rion had created an actual bond between us. Enough of one that I seemed to have access to his light powers. And if that was the case, and if Keph was super-strong in my world, then I could kiss him to share his strength.

While kneeling, his face was at the perfect height, ever-so-slightly below mine. I put my hands to either side of his large head and leaned in.

Then stopped, pulling back.

Kissing on the lips meant so much more to them than it did to me, and I had no idea if this bonding thing was permanent.

Except... that didn't matter. I might barely know these guys and the idea of being magically bound to a stranger should have terrified me, but it didn't. Being with them felt, as Rion had said a moment earlier, right. Still, just because it felt right to me didn't mean it felt right to them.

"Keph—" I didn't know how to ask this.

Will you bond with me?

Can I kiss you?

I want to bond with you. How do you feel about that?

"Yes," he whispered. "Yes, Annie, I will bond with you." His gaze moved past mine and over my shoulder. "If Rion is also well with this?"

Right! I'd already bonded with Rion.

And while he'd said he was fine with Keph teasing me, I didn't know if that made him fine with me also bonding with Keph.

Except it was the only way I was going to be able to save everyone infected in the convention center, hell, the world if I didn't stop this plague here... or in the very least heal as many as I could and get the rest into quarantine before they spread it.

I turned to Rion. "I, ah...."

Jeez. Just rip off the bandage.

"Sorry, but I need to bond with Keph and get his strength," I blurted out. Wow that sounded really utilitarian and was certainly a slap in the face to both of them.

I spun back to Keph, but he didn't seem offended.

Back to Rion.

He seemed fine as well. *Oh, thank God.*

"Sorry, that came out wrong, what I meant was—"

Rion drew close to me—I hadn't really gone that far, there hadn't been much space between him and Rion for me to go—and pressed a finger to my lips to hush me.

"Annie. I know my bond can never claim you, not fully, and I don't expect it to." His look was intense, his body still glowing faintly, though it had faded a bit from earlier. "It's clear this bond between us is more than usual. It's magical. But I know that magic isn't coming from me. It's you, Annie, who've claimed me, taking what's mine."

God, that sounded horrible.

He seemed to see my distress and smiled as he gently brushed a lock of hair away from my cheek. "I want you to take it. I *know* you should. Everything I have is yours if you want it." He knelt as well.

I flushed with the sudden realization that two men were kneeling before me, and we were talking about bonding. Was I about to marry two men? I had no clue. I didn't particularly mind given the men in question. They were kind and generous, if a little strange—although I'm sure I seemed strange to them as well—and it didn't hurt that they were hot as hell.

God, what would everyone say? What would *my family* say?

I didn't care.

"Our bond is forever," Rion continued, his words not striking the kind of fear I'd have expected. "My heart is yours and yours alone, but I can see now, your heart is larger than mine. It can accept more than one bond. I ask only to remain in your heart and in your thoughts."

I stared at him. That sounded a lot like vows.

Fuck.

This was really happening.

I needed to say something in return. "Thank you, Rion. You'll always have a place in my heart and soul." There was little chance I was ever going to forget him, nor our time together.

My dirty mind added another vow: *there will always be a place for you in my pussy, too.*

It wasn't like it wasn't true. And thinking about it only made me more wet down there.

"I formally accept your bond. I know what I did before hurt you, and I'm sorry. You'll always be—" I needed to say something significant here. Oooh! "My first bonded."

I smiled at him and leaned down to kiss him again. His lips were soft and warm and wonderful. As I pulled away, I said, "And I think you're right. I think I can have this sort of bond with more than just one man." Certainly, I didn't feel the sort of singular devotion to him he seemed to feel toward me. Sure, in past relationships I had been singularly devoted to the guy I'd been dating, but this felt different. I felt like there could be— No, that there *should* be more bonds.

He nodded, smiling. "And if it is to be with another, then I couldn't think of a better, truer, more honest and caring man then Keph."

My heart fluttered with joy and desire and certainty, and I turned to Keph. Time for my second set of vows.

Keph was beaming, smiling with acceptance from Rion's words, and that smile grew as he looked at me.

"I, Annie Chambers, would like to bond with you, Kephas… do you have a last name?"

He shrugged. "My clan is Vathia Spiti."

"Kephas Vathia Spiti," I said, letting the name slide over my tongue.

"You make it sound beautiful." His whole being seemed to soften. I could tell he was touched and all I'd done was say his name. "And yes, I will bond with you, Annie Chambers—" His grin deepened. "Goddess extraordinaire."

That brought back some awkward memories. But I still smiled back at him, cupped his face in my hands again, and drew close to kiss him. I had to step to either side of his still-aroused cock, and it brushed against the insides of my thighs and ever-so-faintly against my opening.

All of a sudden, this kiss was making me really, really hot again.

He didn't lean in, didn't force his lips on mine, but was gentle like he always was. Which was good, because where Rion had soft and warm lips, Keph's were firm and unyielding.

The kiss was chaste at first—other than the fact that I was naked and his cock was poised and ready to fill me— but I wanted more from this significant moment, felt it needed to be more, so I brushed my tongue over his lips, teasing them open.

He sighed softly, the sound a low rumble that shivered through my body turning me on even more and wrapped a massive arm around my back and carefully pulled me closer. Even so, I felt the latent strength there, the immense power of which only a meager fraction was used.

His tongue met mine and the kiss deepened, lengthened. I pressed my body to his, savoring the feel of his enormous, hard muscular chest through his sleeveless dress shirt, and a spark snapped through my lips.

I gasped and warmth flooded me, reigniting desire that had been simmering within me since our first encounter.

Oh hell, I wasn't going to be satisfied with just a tease.

I was already wet and ready from Keph's work earlier and he was right there, ready and waiting.

Our lips still locked, I relaxed my legs a little and brushed myself against the massive head of his hard cock. A shudder of need rushed through me, and Keph gasped in a sharp breath. His erection, amazingly, got larger, longer, and harder, and forced me onto my tip-toes to avoid getting impaled.

Holy fuck!

I shifted position, rolling my hips and rubbing myself over his tip. There was no way he'd fit inside me right now—I'd need to be wetter, or have a bottle of lube standing by. But just feeling that impossibly large cock pressed against me, so hard, was enough to tease my opening and hit my clit. I pressed down on it, throwing my arms around Keph's neck to help me keep my balance, while continuing to kiss him.

Keph's breath quickened and he shifted his hand on my back a little higher and pressed the other one against my butt, offering me support but not taking control.

I reached a mini-orgasm just rubbing myself on his

tip. My body trembled and I pressed my forehead to his and released a soft groan. The climax relaxed my muscles and got me even more wet. With a small shudder, which echoed through both of us, his cock inched inside me.

My breath hitched. The promise of another climax quivered through me at him stretching me, promising to fill me completely—hell beyond my limit—and oh-my-fucking-God, it felt incredible.

I slowly tipped my hips forward, inching him in just a little farther, igniting hypersensitive nerves already on the edge and setting off a bigger orgasm. It wasn't the fuck-my-brains-out, stars-flashing-behind-my-lids orgasm I'd had with Rion the other day, but it was still so much more than I'd had in the past.

A long, throaty moan escaped my lips this time and Keph tensed. His tip swelled inside me and he groaned his own soft release, sending more blissful waves washing over me.

Except the waves didn't diminish, they blossomed into a surprising full-body orgasm, that tore out of me with a shuddering scream as his heat and the initial magical heat from our kiss surged inside me.

"Oh, God!" I breathed, when I found my voice again. "That's a kiss I'll never forget."

Keph nodded and shuddered with another surge of his release then finally gasped, "I am yours, Goddess."

And I was his... and Rion's.

Time to see about that. I punched the door behind him, but not very hard—I didn't want to hurt myself—and was shocked when it didn't even sting, even though I'd left an impression of my knuckles in the metal.

Well, damn. I could live with this.

With a groan, Keph carefully withdrew from me, leaving me feeling hollow and unsteady. I glanced around to find my clothes and my gaze landed on Rion.

Fuck! I'd forgotten he was there while lost in the passionate moment with Keph.

But Rion didn't seem put off by our quickie at all. He'd dropped his pants, pulled out his cock, and was stroking it with long, firm strokes. It seemed harsh to leave him there literally with his cock in his hand, so, gripping the shelf beside me to keep my balance, I wobbled the two steps over to him.

I'd just had a mind-blowing kiss. Perhaps I'd give him one as well.

"It's well, Annie, you don't need to—"

I sagged to my knees before him, slid my hand over his hand holding his cock, and wrapped my mouth around the end.

"Oh," he gasped and I grinned up at him. His eyes had grown wide, his pupils fully dilated while his breath had jumped to ragged and fast and his body trembled.

I nudged his hand away so I could fully take over, running my hand down his length to his base while swirling my tongue over his tip.

"Oh, Hermes!" He grabbed the shelf beside him, his cock growing harder in my grip.

I drew my hand up his length and back down, mindful of my newly found strength, and took more of him in my mouth.

"Annie, I—"

Another stroke and this time my lips followed my hand, taking him fully into my mouth.

"Annie," he groaned and his body stiffened as his salty release rushed into my mouth. Oh, yeah, he'd been well primed.

I bit back a silly grin. Now, we'd all had something.

And I felt strong enough to take on the world.

CHAPTER 4

ANNIE

My body thrummed with energy as I used a wad of paper towels—stollen from the shelf beside Rion—to clean up then started to get dressed. I felt like... there wasn't a comparison. I'd never felt so self-assured and confident. Being with these two men, at the same time, seeing how much they wanted me, had filled me with so much love and certainty. I was on top of the world... which was good, because I still had a convention center full of people to cure.

I finished dressing, feeling refreshed and ready to work. Turning to the guys, they too were ready to go, and looked God-damned sexy.

Another thrill rushed through me. They were bonded to me. Both of them. And had shown me just how much they desired me. And the best part was that I knew this wasn't a dream!

"Ready to go?" I asked.

"Are you?" Rion replied.

I nodded. "Let's do this."

We left the storage room in time to find one of the security men running toward us. "Everything's been shut down," he called out. "People are being kept in the larger rooms and a few hallways. The police have arrived and are taking care of things outside." The man actually looked worried. It wasn't the leader from before, just some poor young man in the wrong place.

With all the poise of my newfound energy I smiled reassuringly as I approached him. Reaching up I cupped his cheek to check to see if he was infected. He didn't have the disease.

I blinked.

I shouldn't have known that right away. Before, I'd had to actively search for the disease in someone, but I'd known the second I'd touched him that he wasn't infected.

Guess my new found ability was growing.

"Everything is well," I said calmly. I made a show of looking in his eyes and opening his mouth to look inside. "You're well and haven't contracted anything. Keep away from people for the moment if you can. It's spread through skin contact and the onset is quick." I didn't know if it was quick, but if it wasn't, there was no logical way I'd know if he was infected or not by just looking at him.

He seemed to relax a little, thankfully not questioning how my explanation didn't really make sense, medically speaking. "Thank you, ma'am."

I'd never really been a 'ma'am' before and wasn't sure how I felt about that. I wasn't old enough to be a ma'am, but ma'am's were in charge and that's what I needed to be right now.

"Take me to where the people are gathered so I can take a look at them."

He nodded, turned on his heel, and led us out of the large room and into the hall.

"You calmed him down quickly," Rion said.

"It helps when I feel calm myself." I stopped and let the two men flanking me pass me a little. They turned back. "Thank you, both of you." I met the level gaze of each of them in turn. "Rion, Keph, I know this is going to sound crazy, but I love you." It felt right in my soul to say it even though I barely knew these men. "I don't know how this is all going to work out once we're finished here, but I know I love you."

All my life I'd thought true love was something between two people, and a fairy tale at that. Yet I had a new certainty now. True love was something that could be shared and was completely real. I had no clue what that really meant, but I needed to let them know how I felt.

Both men smiled, then simultaneously glanced at each other. Something, some unsaid notion passed between them and they both nodded.

"I love you too, Annie," Keph said softly.

"As do I," Rion added. "We'll... work out the details of this odd relationship later. Know that we are with you, for whatever you need."

Whatever I needed. Oh, I was well aware of that. They'd just shown me. And I was looking forward to *more* later.

"Good," I said, and hurried after the security guard while the guys fell in a step slightly behind me and to either side.

The guard led us to a large hall filled with stalls where security had done a good job organizing people. They were lined up around the outside wall, then in a single file row down each of the aisles between stalls.

Stopping, I turned to Keph and reached for his hand. That large, hard, yet gentle hand engulfed mine, and I felt his power fill me once again. This bond thing was amazing.

"Let's do this!" I said and turned to the first row of people.

Time blurred and I focused solely on checking people. One person then the next. I couldn't look at how many I'd checked or how many were left. I just had to keep going. One foot in front of the other.

When I grew weary, Keph was there for another surge of energy, and I kept going until I stepped away from a tall, skinny man in some kind of plastic, home-made body armor, and realized there wasn't anyone else.

There'd been close to two hundred people infected, but thankfully they'd all been in the initial stages and were easily healed. Still, healing two hundred people had been exhausting even with Keph's help.

With a heavy sigh, I turned to find the lead security guard in my face flanked by men with FBI in big bold letters on their jackets.

Well, fuck.

"Special Agent Annie Chambers was it?" the security

guard said with a sneer. "Seems the FBI has no record of an agent by that name."

"Great, you can arrest me now." I held my hands out, wrists together. Even without looking, I could tell Rion and Keph were confused. Perhaps it was some effect of our bond that let me know what they were feeling. "But I wasn't wrong about the bio-terrorist attack. Luckily those here are clean, but you take an infectious disease specialist through the other halls and check for people with small black spots on their skin. They'd be hard to find at this early stage, but those people are still highly contagious and should be quarantined from everyone else and anyone else should be checked hourly to see if such spots develop."

The man's bluster deflated just a little at my calm confidence. "Who are you?"

"Annie Chambers, goddess." I tilted my head just a little to the right and offered him a dazzling smile. I knew that line would probably land me in a loony-bin, but I couldn't help myself. Besides Keph and Rion would protect me. Just to be really messed-up, I made myself glow.

The security guard's eyes bulged just a little.

"Now, are you going to have someone look at the other halls, or are you going to let me through so I can heal them?"

I didn't think the guard or the two FBI agents quite knew what to do with a self-assured, glowing woman flanked by two guys: one who looked like a model and the other like a small mountain.

I walked forward, and the security guard moved aside.

The FBI agents, looked at each other, shrugged then also moved aside.

"Thanks, boys," I said casually, my heart racing a mile a minute, my entire being filled with bravado and justified bluster. I could get used to this.

Behind me I heard one of the FBI-guys probably on a phone. "Ah... yeah... can we get an infectious disease specialist out here?" A pause. "Also, maybe someone from the paranormal division."

That was a thing?

Cool.

"What do we do now?" Keph asked. "Stay and heal more or let them deal with it?"

"I'm going to stay until someone kicks me out." Or I collapsed from exhaustion. Whichever came first. "On to the next room." I indicated our way with an assured straight-arm point.

Rion chuckled. "I take it people in your world aren't used to seeing a goddess."

"Nope."

"Those men looked like they were going to run when you started glowing." His laughter deepened and I joined him. For the moment at least, I felt good.

I began examining the people who'd been lined up in the next hall, but about a third of the way through, more people in FBI uniforms arrived, three of whom—two burly men and a lean woman in a lab coat—came to me.

The woman, with sharp green eyes, pale brown hair pulled back in a professional bun, and carrying a bag with the strap slung over her shoulder, cleared her throat. "Uh, excuse me?"

I smiled at her as I moved on from one person to the next. "Yes?"

"You're the uh... healer?"

"Yep."

"Might I... watch?"

"As long as you don't get in my way."

The woman nodded.

True to her word, she, and the two larger men with her, simply watched me for a while. The next seven people I inspected weren't infected, but the one after that was.

"Hey," I called over to her. "What's your name?"

"Janice," she said moving a little closer. "Yours?"

"Annie Chambers." She looked like she was about to ask more, but I cut her off. "See these spots?" I said indicating the small black dots on the face of the young man in front of me.

"Yes." Janice looked closer. "This is the disease?"

"Yes."

"Might I take a sample?" she asked.

I didn't know if that was a good idea, but if the authorities came across someone who was infected without me, they'd need to know everything they could about it. "Just be really careful with it."

"I will." She pulled a long swab from her bag, broke open the packaging and took a sample from the man's mouth. Then, with another swab, took a sample from one of the black spots. Once done, she put the swabs in sealable plastic bags that then went in another bio-hazard pouch.

I turned to the man, whose eyes were now wide with fear.

"Don't worry," I said. "I'm going to heal you."

Which, if I really thought about it, was crazy. If I didn't know what I knew, I would have thought I was crazy.

But I touched his face and let my power seep into him, and the fear in his eyes changed to awe as he felt my power flow into him. It didn't take much energy, either that or I was getting used to this, and the small spots faded from the man's skin.

"Oh, wow. I didn't think I felt bad, but... wow. I feel great now!" he gasped.

I turned to Janice, who was also wide-eyed with awe.

"All gone," I said.

"How...?" Janice opened her mouth then closed it as if she were at a loss for words.

I shrugged. "I don't really know. I shouldn't be able to do this, but I can. If you ask either of these two," I said, indicating Rion and Keph, "they'll tell you I'm a goddess. Right now, I can't refute them."

"Uh-hunh." Janice looked at me like I had two heads... sort of. It was a strange look, as if she didn't want to believe what she was seeing, but was also coming to terms with my 'two heads.'

She shrugged after a moment. "Go about your work then," she said and turned to the two bewildered men behind her. "I can't explain it," she whispered. "Faith healer maybe?"

I went back to work, and Janice and her crew kept watch from a distance.

When I was done, I stepped back into the hall to go to the next room only to find a squad of men wearing black body armor pointing their guns at me. They looked like they were staring down a rabid rhino.

Keph laid a heavy, reassuring hand on my shoulder, his thumb rubbing gentle circles on the back of my neck. It was a comforting touch and made me just a little warm, but also renewed my connection with him, giving me more strength.

"Annie?" Rion asked.

I was about to ask these men what they wanted... when my phone rang.

The FBI guys all flinched and tensed, and, with my hands open, palms up to show I wasn't armed, I slowly reached into my pocket and drew out my phone.

I swiped to activate the call and put it to my ear. "Yes?"

"We have a problem," Del said.

A squad of FBI guys had their guns pointed at me. That... was a bit of an understatement.

CHAPTER 5

HYPERION

Annie was very still, but also smiling. I wasn't sure how much of Keph's abilities she might have taken from their bond, just as I was uncertain how bright she could become using my light. There were a lot of unknowns floating around, but I didn't want to risk her getting hurt. And right now, with these men pointing their weapons at us there was a good chance she would be.

I edged a little closer to her. I didn't know how those strange looking weapons worked, but I'd put myself between her and danger. My vow—my *bond*—demanded it.

"Yes?" Annie said into the device she held against her cheek. What had she called it again? A *phone*?

"Oh? Really? So do I. What's yours?"

No one moved. Apparently, these men with the letters F B I on their strange, padded armor were willing to let Annie talk.

"Well, fuckity-fuck-fuck!" Annie hissed, too quiet for the men to hear and without losing her smile. "And we have no idea where they are? ... Of course. Well, stay with her and stay hidden. ... My problem? Oh, just some men with guns. ... Yes, those things that hurt you from a distance. No! Del, stay where you are with the *naiad*. She can't be set free. Maybe we can get more information out of her. ... Yeah, bye." She removed the *phone* from her ear and sighed as she slowly put it away. Turning to the men with the guns she asked, "How can I help you?"

"Annie Chambers?" someone called out.

"That would be me."

"You're under arrest for impersonating a federal agent and inciting chaos."

"Sounds fair," she whispered.

"Wait!" the woman who'd been watching Annie work said as she hurried out of the room we'd just been in. "Put those guns down and don't arrest her. Who's in charge here?"

This began a heated conversation in hushed voices between that woman—also with the F B I letters on her uniform, half hidden under her long white coat—and another man.

The man's voice rose enough for me to hear a derisive scoff, then, "Yeah, right, and I'm the president."

Janice spoke louder. "I saw it with my own eyes."

"Then your eyes are failing."

"Ah... excuse me?" Annie said. She had her hands up and out in front of her and slowly inched toward them even though a few of the men still had their weapons pointed at her.

Keph and I moved with her, and I knew he was just as ready to protect her as I was.

"What?" the man snapped, his voice thick with exasperation.

"If you're looking for proof that I'm some supernatural entity, I can give that to you." Annie's smile deepened. She seemed so confident, different than when we'd met her. Well, no, she'd seemed confident when we'd first met her, but she'd thought everything was a dream. Once she'd realized the truth, she'd seemed so small and uncertain and it had broken my heart.

"A supernatural what?" the man asked.

"Entity. Goddess to be exact."

"Yeah, right!" he huffed.

"Okay, here goes." She began to glow.

The man's eyes widened with shock. "Fuck me!" he gasped then his expression snapped back to hard skepticism. "That's just some trick of the light."

Annie shrugged. "Fine, just remember, you asked for this."

She stepped in and punched the man in the stomach, hitting him square in the middle of his armored chest. He flew back a dozen feet, hit the slick, shiny floor, and skidded another dozen feet before stopping.

A loud crack exploded around us and Annie flinched and grabbed her forehead. "Ow! Hey!"

My pulse froze and I grabbed her arm to pull her to safety, but she glanced at me, looking fine, and the rest of me froze.

I didn't know what had happened. She had a wound on her forehead smaller than my smallest fingernail, that wept a small trickle of blood, and her gaze had dropped to a small deformed ball of metal in her hand. Even as I watched, the wound stopped bleeding and faded to nothing.

"Well, if I didn't believe it before, I do now," Janice said in awe, as Keph jerked in front of Annie, shielding her with his massive body from any more attacks.

Annie used that distraction to turn to me. "Bring out your wings," she whispered.

I did.

I felt the familiar rush of power and whispered pain as my wings sprung from my shoulder blades and flared out on either side of me. Except, too late, I remembered I still wore the jacket Annie had borrowed for me, and they tore through the fabric. So much for that.

"I also come with an angel," Annie said jovially. She'd called me that before. I didn't know what that was, but everyone else seemed to. There were gasps and exclamations from the group. "Now, Janice," Annie said, turning to the woman. "You seem reasonable. Is it okay if I go and heal some more people?"

The woman stammered for a moment, eyes wide, staring at me before she nodded. "Ah, yes, go ahead. I'll take care of this."

"You're such a dear, thank you!" Annie headed down the hall to go to the next room and Keph and I followed.

When she got to the FBI man she'd punched, who was still lying on the floor, she knelt next to him. He seemed stunned still and struggled to catch his breath.

"Sorry about that," Annie said, and laid a hand on his cheek. His eyes went wide with fear. "Oooh, really sorry, wow, so many broken ribs! I don't know my own strength yet. Here—" The man's fear changed to awe and he drew in a full, deep breath. "Better?"

He nodded.

Annie patted his cheek. "Great! Gotta go heal some other people." She rose and moved off.

Keph glared down at the still prone man and offered a low threatening growl that frightened even me.

I looked back as we moved on. The man was staring at us, his expression a mix of shock and confusion and awe. It seemed we were getting a lot of those looks. I waved, and released my wings, letting them melt into nothing as we continued on.

"What did Del say?" Keph asked as we entered yet another large room filled with people. I wasn't sure how many Annie had checked and healed so far, I'd lost count. At least a few hundred if not a thousand or more, and while she looked in good health, I was still worried that she was going to keep going until she collapsed, just like the last time.

"Apparently the *naiad* let slip that two of her duplicates are still out there, spreading disease," Annie said. "I'm betting they've already fled the convention center, but just in case, keep an eye out for her. There isn't much we can do about it now, though." She glanced out the door into the hall and frowned.

I shrugged out of my ruined jacket and turned to see what concerned her. Janice was running to catch up with us. Her two escorts flanking her, but thankfully the men in the strange black fabric armor had dispersed.

Janice stopped, a bit out of breath. "Ah, miss— Annie — Goddess?" she said, stumbling over her own words.

"Yes, Janice?" Annie said.

"I'm to be your liaison for now."

"That's great, and while you're here, can you put out an A.P.B.—or whatever you call them?"

Janice frowned. "Ah... sure. For who?"

"The woman who caused all this. She's ahh... triplets! Yes, triplets. We caught one of them, but the other two are still out there. They shouldn't be too hard to find. They have blue skin. Light blue, like a summer sky."

"What if they take off their make-up?" Janice asked.

"It's not make-up. They actually have blue skin." Annie laughed. "Actually, we'd need to be worried if they *found* make-up and knew what to do with it. Oh, and be careful, she can turn to water and slip away at will."

"Turn to..." Janice's frown deepened and I could see questions form in her eyes before she gave a tight nod of acceptance and forced a smile. "Right, will do, thanks Goddess Annie." She turned to one of the men behind her. "Call it in."

"I can't—" the man said. "No one will believe me."

"Just call it in," Janice pressed.

The man reached for his *phone,* his expression clear that he thought it was pointless and Janice turned back to us.

"Anything else?" she asked.

"That's it for now, thank you."

"Whatever you need," Janice said, though she sounded just a little less certain than she had a few moments ago.

Annie moved through the next room, taking energy from Keph more and more often. By the time she was done, Keph was looking weary, something I'd never seen before. It was a testament to the massive amount of work Annie was doing and the energy she was expending.

The two of them rested for a bit in the next hall, Keph gathering Annie in his arms and holding her close while they sat on the floor, and I took Janice aside to speak to her.

"Do you know how many more people there are to heal?" I asked.

Janice stared at my bare chest for a long time before blinking, as if she'd just realized I'd asked her a question.

"Ah... what? People? Oh, right, sorry." She pulled out her *phone* and activated it, scrolling through some images. "It looks like there were a total of twenty-three thousand, seven-hundred-and-forty-three people here when we quarantined the place."

It was my turn to stare at her like she'd stared at me with my wings out. "That's— That's so many! How many have we looked at so far?"

"About seven thousand."

My jaw dropped again. I knew it was a lot, but that was more than I'd expected. And at the same time still only about a third of what needed to be done. This was going to take forever.

"I know," Janice said softly. She looked back at Annie resting in Keph's arms. "I don't know how she's come this far, doing what she's doing. Not that I have any clue what she's doing, but even just following her, watching her, staying on my feet for this long, is exhausting."

"Thank you, Janice," I said and slowly returned to the other two.

"What was that about?" Annie asked. She was recovering quickly, but I couldn't say the same for Keph, who still looked weary.

"I asked how many people there were left to see."

"And?"

I did the math quickly. "Roughly sixteen thousand."

Annie nodded slowly. "Fuck."

"Yeah."

"How many have we gone through?" she asked.

"About seven thousand."

"Ah, okay, good, good." She nodded again as if that was the only action she could think of doing then released a heavy sigh. "This is going to take forever."

"That's what I was thinking."

Annie forced a smile and slowly rose. "Better get to it then."

Gods, she was amazing.

CHAPTER 6

ANNIE

I HURT IN PLACES WHERE I'D NEVER HURT BEFORE. Someone had brought me food several times, one of them a breakfast, and I assumed that meant I'd worked through the night. There were windows somewhere in the building, but I'd long since stopped paying attention and had no clue what time it was. All I knew was... I was finally done!

I slumped in a hallway, sitting against a wall, staring at the opposite wall but not really seeing it. With an earth-shaking *thud*, Keph sagged to the floor next to me. He was in rough shape.

I'd pulled everything I dared from him, and I knew he'd have given more if I'd asked, but I was worried what that might do to him. I recovered quickly with my healing ability, but Keph... he was much more sluggish than usual and I didn't know how long it would take for his energy to come back.

"Done," Keph said heavily.

"As if you did anything," I said, softly elbowing him

and trying to be playful. With the power I took from him, he actually swayed a little from my nudge... or maybe I was just that strong and hadn't fully realized it.

He turned to me, one brow raised. "Really?"

"It was a joke."

He smiled faintly, then thumped his head back against the wall so hard the wall cracked.

Rion glanced at us. He was pacing, full of nervous energy, but I didn't know if I could take strength from him the way I did with Keph. I'd assumed I could only take the ability associated with the man, nothing more. And while I was curious, I didn't have the energy to try. I'd have to experiment with that later.

Everything would come later.

Which reminded me. I needed to check in with Del and Aethan.

I took out my phone, swiped it on, and hit the last number called. It rang for a while then Del answered.

"Annie? Is that you?" he asked, his voice filled with concern. "Are you well?"

"Well enough, yes. Thought I'd check in with you. How's the *naiad*?"

"Thank the gods," Del said, relief flooding his voice. "The *naiad* hasn't said much in... it's been a long time. We're getting hungry here."

Right. Fuck. They were hiding somewhere in this complex of buildings, waiting while I'd healed all those people. And even if they'd tried to go out and find some food, they had no money.

"Aethan stole us some food yesterday, but we don't want to push our luck."

"Stole?" I didn't want to know from where. "Where are you guys. I'll come to you. I'm tired, but we should regroup and figure out our next steps."

"I honestly have no clue where we are. Some closet deep in the bowels of one of the many buildings here."

Great. Well, they were well hidden at least.

"Do you remember how you got there?"

"Aethan says he does."

I rose, slowly, leaning against the wall to keep my balance. "Okay. Let me make my way back to where we left you, then you can guide us. We'll come to you and—"

Agent Janice walked around the corner at the end of the hall and headed toward us. A small exhausted part of me said I should probably ask what her last name was, but the rest of me was too tired to care. And really, it wasn't that important at the moment.

"I'll call you back when we're ready." I hung up to some clipped reply from Del that I didn't quite catch.

"Does the FBI need more from Amazing Goddess Annie?" I asked, my voice weak and wobbly, like the rest of me.

"Once we track down the last blue-woman you told us about, we may need you to heal more of the city. If that's... possible? You look tired."

"Little known fact, gods have their limits, and I've reached mine."

"Ah. Well, can we call you when we—?"

My brain finally caught up with what she'd said a moment ago. "The last woman? You found one of them?"

"Yes, and we have her in custody."

Wow. "You actually managed to capture her, even

when she can turn to water." I was surprised and impressed. I figured they might find her, but I hadn't expected them to actually capture her.

"Indeed." Janice smirked. "No one believed me when I told them that. But they tracked one down and that's exactly what she did. But I guess she didn't count on how cold it was outside and she didn't get far, nearly freezing, so she turned back into a person. The agents then deployed some... ah... innovative techniques to capture her."

"Innovative techniques?" This, I had to hear.

"A... ah... fish tank. They've restrained her in a large fish tank and are carrying her around in it." Janice shrugged. "Things I'd never thought I'd say. If you'd told me a week ago this was how today would go, I wouldn't have believed you."

"I have that effect." I gave my winningest smile. It was probably wobbly too. "I have to go. If you need to reach me, call me." I told her my number then turned away to go meet Del and Aethan.

"I'll text you my number in case you need it," Janice said.

I wobbled a few steps farther and Rion rushed forward to help me, while Keph staggered to his feet.

"Annie?" Janice said, her voice soft.

I glanced back at her.

"Thank you." She bowed her head as if I really was a goddess... and well, maybe I actually was. I didn't know, but the reverence made me slightly uncomfortable. "I don't know about anyone else, but I'll say a prayer to

Goddess Annie every night for a while. What you did today... and yesterday... was a miracle."

I smiled again, not sure what to say to that then continued walking away, with Rion helping and Keph, looking like he wanted to also help but needing the wall to stay upright.

We moved slowly and eventually found our way back to the room where we'd captured the *naiad*. I called Del and he led us—with only a few dead-ends and wrong turns—to them. They were indeed in a storage room with shelves and stacked chairs. Just looking at it made my face heat. After my escapades—I guess it was yesterday now—I had a completely different view of storage rooms.

"Save us some time and just tell me where your duplicates are," I said to the *naiad*, too tired to beat around the bush. "I'm sure you have some way of knowing their location."

"I don't." She flashed a victorious smile even though she'd been captured and was probably hungry. "They know where I am and can return to me whenever they wish or if I call them."

Call them, hunh? That was a slip, and from the sudden crack in her smile, she knew it as soon as she'd said it.

"Then call them. 'Cause I'm tired and if you don't, I'll have one of my big friends here crack your head open like a melon. Do you have melons in your world?" I asked Del.

He nodded.

"Yep, like a melon," I said to her. "I'm sure that would deal with your duplicates, too."

Her eyes widened and Keph growled on cue.

Good Keph.

"Fine! Yes, I'll call them in." Her smile returned. "But they've been out there for over a day. The damage is done."

Which I already knew. But I'd deal with that later... if I could deal with it—

No. I *would*. I was a goddess after all.

But the first thing to take care of was stopping the duplicates from continuing to actively spread the disease.

The *naiad's* smile weakened then slid into a frown and a few minutes later she hissed a sharp curse. "Akheloios! One of my duplicates has died."

That wasn't too much of a surprise. I wasn't sure what her 'return call' was like, but if the duplicates couldn't resist it, then the one in custody probably had tried to escape and been shot and killed.

"The other one is coming," the *naiad* huffed. "It might take a while."

Great. I didn't want to keep standing around, I wanted to go home to bed, but I also wasn't going to leave until the duplicates weren't running around creating more problems. Sure, the disease was likely already being spread by humans now, but they weren't actively trying to spread it like the *naiad* and her duplicates had.

While we waited, I tried to figure out what the hell I was going to do with her. My initial thought was to hand her over to Janice but I had a feeling that would create more problems. I felt like I could trust Janice—don't ask me why—but that didn't mean everyone Janice worked with and everyone the *naiad* might come in contact with could be trusted.

It was bad enough one evil man from my world had learned about having powers in my guys' world. I couldn't risk more people finding out. That had disaster written all over it. Even if they didn't have a power that they could manipulate to influence my world like Disease Man had, they'd still have power in the other world and could terrorize those people.

No. The only safe answer for everyone was for the *naiad* to return to her world and then hope Janice wouldn't think it smart to question the decision of a goddess.

I really wanted to be able to hand the *naiad* over to whatever authorities there were in the guys' world, but I didn't really have the energy to make that happen and what energy I managed to recover after getting some rest should be put toward figuring out how to deal with the plague in my world.

Not to mention the second we stepped through the alley wall the *naiad* would be able to turn to water—since the other world's natural shifting abilities worked in both worlds—but Del would lose his ability to control her.

And I wasn't going to hope that Disease Man hadn't mentioned the fact that people only had powers in the other world and not their own. I had to assume that she knew and the second we crossed over, the guys would lose their magic and she'd be able to escape.

Crap. I wished I'd been thinking about this when I'd first told Janice to catch the duplicates. But I'd been so focused on containing the disease and healing everyone,

I hadn't been thinking about what would happen afterward.

While I thought, Rion told Del and Aethan what had happened with the security guards, the FBI, Janice, and about healing everyone in the convention center who'd been infected—the last part making the *naiad* deflate even more and glare at me.

An hour later, the last remaining duplicate staggered in, looking exhausted and wearing rags. The *naiad* held out her hand as if to hug her and the duplicate stepped into her embrace and the two merged into one.

"It's done," the *naiad* said. "Now what?"

"Now we put you back in your world."

She scowled. Guess she didn't like that idea. I didn't care.

Rion met my gaze and I could see the question in his eyes, but I didn't want to say anything about what I'd decided in that last hour while in front of the *naiad*. But then he gave a tight nod, all question vanishing from his gaze, as if he'd come to the same conclusion I had—and in a fraction of the time. Well, I was exhausted from having healed *thousands* of people.

We covered her up in some of my layers, snuck out the closest exit, headed away from where the FBI guys had been, and hailed a cab.

Luckily this one was a mini-van and big enough to take all six of us. It still groaned under Keph's weight, but it got us to the alley across town.

I got to the wall, put my hand on it, and Keph pushed the *naiad* through.

And that was that.

It wasn't great or perfect, but it was the best I could come up with.

Now I needed to sleep.

Then we'd find the man behind all of this, the one with disease powers who could cross worlds like I could, and then I'd somehow heal an entire city.

Sure. Easy.

CHAPTER 7

DELPHON

WE'D ARRIVED BACK AT ANNIE'S RESIDENCE TIRED AND hungry. The man who Annie had healed in the alley when we'd first been searching for the *naiad* and who she'd said could stay in her residence for a couple of nights had been there. But he hadn't wanted to stay with a group of strangers, and Annie had given the man some green papers and wished him well before sending him off.

While we'd been waiting for the naiad's duplicate to return, we'd gotten the whole story about what had happened to Annie, Rion, and Keph after Aethan and I had taken and hidden with the *naiad*. It was... mind-boggling and there was still a lot left to do before the whole situation was over.

The trouble was, neither Aethan nor I knew this place well enough to go anywhere or do anything to help out while Annie recovered from healing all those people, so, we waited.

Luckily Annie had bought some food on our way

back to her home, so at least we weren't starving any longer.

Now Keph was asleep, sprawled on Annie's common room floor, and Annie was in her bed, also slumbering, while Rion slept on the floor next to her. Aethan and I had slept in shifts, watching the *naiad* in turns while we'd waited for Annie and the others to deal with the guards and then the infected people. So we weren't that tired now. I tried to think, while Aethan paced, moving normally for a few steps then zipping forward, hard to see before reappearing somewhere else still just pacing. I didn't know if it was helping him to calm down or not.

I, too, tried to find some calm, but alas, it was fleeting, slipping from my mental grip the second I thought I had some, my thoughts constantly jumping back to what had happened and about Keph and Rion and their new relationship with Annie.

She'd mentioned—glossing over the details—that she'd bonded with Keph, and how she was able to borrow abilities from those she'd bonded with.

Which was amazing and unheard of and made her look more and more like the goddess we'd all initially thought her to be.

And no matter what I tried, I couldn't help but imagine her kiss, those soft lips on mine, her body pressed close, arms and legs entwined—

I tried to shove those thoughts aside. They weren't helping. They only made me more uncomfortable... although not as uncomfortable as I could have been if I still had my pants on. We'd disrobed as soon as we'd returned to Annie's place, feeling much more at home with nothing on—which, given the customs of Annie's world might have also explained why the old man hadn't wanted to stay with us.

With a heavy sigh, I changed positions on the long couch from sitting and watching Aethan's fast-slow stuttering movements, to putting my feet up on one end and resting my head on the other and—

I started awake. Someone had called my name.

Apparently, I'd fallen asleep and had been dreaming of Annie and me, unencumbered by clothes, frolicking in the sea.

I rubbed my hands over my face, disappointed that I'd been woken and glanced at Aethan who was looking at me with a wide grin.

"Sleep well?" He jerked his chin toward a tired looking Rion coming out of Annie's room, which sent a spike of jealousy twisting in my gut even though I knew he'd slept on the floor. "The goddess wants to see us."

My jealousy snapped to hope for a moment, but I quickly shoved the feelings down. This was most likely *not* what I hoped it would be.

I stood and Rion took my place on the couch, falling asleep before I'd even closed the door to Annie's room behind me.

She sat in bed with a glint of something—mischief perhaps?—in her eyes, looking mostly refreshed. It stunned me to see how fast she recovered, but then she was a goddess, or as close to a goddess as someone could be, and it made sense that she recovered faster than normal.

She'd pulled the blankets high on her chest, but I

could tell from her bare arms and shoulders that she wasn't wearing anything beneath them... or maybe that's what I wanted to think. And even if it wasn't true, the idea was a strong enough tease that my already semi-hard erection from my dream grew harder, which was strange and amazing and wonderful. Women in my world didn't wear much clothing if any and while I'd been attracted to and had reacted to many women, I had never reacted like this with anyone but Annie. Gods, she was beautiful with her gold eyes, red-blond hair, and the mysterious spots on her face and arms.

"We need to... talk," she said with a coy little smile that made my heart skip a beat.

Was I right? Were my dreams about to come true?

I glanced at Aethan. He'd caught her smile too and was trying to hide a hopeful grin and doing a terrible job at it.

"Yes, Annie?" Aethan said. "We're here for whatever you need."

"That," she said softly, "is exactly what I was hoping you'd say." She let the covers fall away from her, and, as I'd suspected, was wearing nothing, giving us a stunning view of her full, inviting breasts.

She slid her legs out from under the blankets over the side of the bed, and they too were bare. Then she rose, letting the coverings fall away and stood before us nude and proud and beautiful. Gods, but she was amazing!

Her gaze locked onto mine and seemed to hold my very soul. Then, she slid her attention to Aethan, capturing him for a moment as well. Finally, she let out a heavy sigh. Her coy smile slipped away and she lost a hint of her glory.

"I'm afraid," she said softly, "that what we faced these last few days is only the beginning. Disease Man is still out there and I can't shake the feeling that he's not the only one like me who can travel between worlds. That, and there are more people, most likely a lot more people, who'll need to be healed."

The memory of her healing the people of Masia until she passed out and her gray-skinned, exhausted look after healing everyone in the convention center flashed through me. She didn't know when to stop and would hurt herself trying to heal everyone.

"Annie, this isn't your responsibility," I said. "You— All of us, we're not heroes. We're normal people who happen to know of a way to cross between two worlds. I don't think—"

"You're wrong, Del." Her stunning gold eyes grew hard with determination. "One of my boyfriends dragged me along to a superhero movie a long time ago. I don't remember much of it, but there's one line that keeps coming back to me. Something about 'having power means having a responsibility.' And I have power. I might be the only one with the power to stop this before it turns into a disaster. Or—" Her gaze dipped down and a soft flush colored her pale cheeks. "Or I could have the power if..."

She could have the power?

My thoughts stuttered. She'd mentioned she'd gained the powers that both Rion and Keph had gained in this world after she'd bonded with them. Something I'd never heard of happening before. Bonding, as much as it was a significant thing in my world, wasn't anything magical. It was highly symbolic, but not actually binding.

A warmth blossomed in my chest and I realized what she was trying to say and why she stood before us naked.

"You wish to bond with us, to gain greater power," I said.

"Not just power," she said, her voice soft. "Yes, I think I'll need to be stronger to face what's coming, but also—" Her flush deepened and seeped down her neck, making the spots on her skin stand out. "I don't know how to explain it. It doesn't make sense. I barely know you four, but I *know* I'm supposed to bond with you." She took two long strides to stand before me, so close her nipples brushed across my chest. My erect cock pressed against her belly and she stared up into my eyes.

I'd thought myself fully aroused before, but my cock grew harder and my balls tightened. Annie's eyes darted down and she bit her lip. Her breath picked up and she leaned closer, pressing her breasts to my chest.

"I don't know how or why you four came into my life, but my soul hurt when I sent you back to your world. I didn't realize the truth until I bonded with Keph, but I'm supposed to be bonded with you. I don't want to imagine my life without you. All of you." Her voice grew husky and desire burned in her eyes.

The urge to take her right there, lift her onto my cock, bring her pleasure as she claimed me with her kiss, surged through me, but Aethan shifted beside me, reminding me that we weren't alone.

Judging from his full erection, he was probably

having similar thoughts. And as I thought that, the image of Annie in my arms, riding my cock returned, except this time Aethan was there, entering her from behind as we thrust into her together.

The vision was gone in an instant, but I was only more aroused at the thought of sharing Annie with the man who was like a brother to me, which made me realize just how true her words were.

I didn't particularly like the idea of sharing a woman, particularly a bonded mate. And yet the idea of Annie bonding with the others didn't bother me at all. In fact, crazy as it was, the idea of her *not* bonding with them felt wrong.

Annie's gaze dipped to Aethan's cock and she gave a light laugh. "I see you're ready. Give me a moment and I'll be with you shortly. But first—" She looked back to me, capturing me with her golden gaze. "There's a process to this. Delphon of Galniosia, will you accept a bond with me? There's no going back from this. I don't know how your bonds usually work, but this one, I believe, is truly binding. I won't do that to you unless it's what you want."

My heart skipped a beat.

"I—"

Did I want this?

I mean, by Hades, yes, I wanted Annie. She was the most wonderous woman I'd ever met: enigmatic and powerful yet still somehow vulnerable. She was so very different, in nearly every way, from the women I'd known before. The trouble was... I really liked being with women.

I'd shared a lot about myself with my friends, these

three men, but I'd kept one big secret from them. I spoke often of the 'great prince' of my kingdom in my reports, but had never mentioned that *I* was that prince.

I'd never wanted the responsibility of being a king. I'd loved my position of privilege, but didn't want the responsibilities that came with it. I knew that was selfish and irresponsible, but for the longest time, I'd just accepted that was who I was: a selfish and irresponsible prince, who loved how women flocked to my position of power in the hopes of winning me and becoming the next queen.

I'd loved that life... and hated it.

I'd loved the many trysts with triton noblewomen, but hated that I always felt I was lying to them. It was one of the reasons I'd waylaid our emissary to these meetings in Masia and taken his place. I wanted to be free. I wanted to have a moment in my life where I wasn't a prince, to see what that was like. And it turned out I loved it. I was still a bounder who loved to dally with any woman who'd have me, but there were no perceived promises to them. I wasn't a prince, just a man.

If I accepted this bond with Annie, I'd have to give up all that. Everything. The women, and probably my title. The title would be easy to leave, though the privilege that came with it would be tough to abandon. But I'd live. I liked being just Delphon the triton.

Yet the women...

Didn't matter. They'd been a way to bide my time while I'd been waiting for Annie. I just hadn't realized that until now and I knew, without a doubt, I'd give up all the women in two worlds— in all the worlds, for the one in front of me.

"Yes. I want this."

Her smile grew and she brought her arms up behind my head to urge me down as she rose on her toes to press her lips to mine.

The kiss was everything I thought and hoped it would be, soft and yielding, yet hot and passionate. Teeth nipped, lips pressed, tongues dueled. And she claimed me. I felt it deep in my soul, like a powerful wave sweeping through me as an incredible magic bound me to her with an unbreakable connection. It, along with her kiss, stole my breath.

I grabbed her waist, lifting her, so she wouldn't need to crane her neck back. She wrapped her legs around me and deepened the kiss. Her hips rocked and swayed, and she ground herself against my cock captured between us, making my pulse roar in my ears.

Then she drew back, her golden eyes shining. "I accept your bond," she whispered.

I couldn't move, mesmerized by her eyes and her glorious smile. "And I accept yours." I kept her there, close, my desire growing until her smile turned playful.

"You need to put me down, Del, so I can talk with Aethan."

Oh... right. It wouldn't be fair to Aethan for him to have his moment with her while she was still in my arms. That would be awkward in so many ways. He'd let me have her to myself for our binding, I could give him the same consideration.

I set her down, but she didn't move away quickly.

Instead, she grabbed the base of my erection, hard, squeezing as she roughly slid her hand up to the tip, then off.

I shuddered with a minor orgasm, barely keeping myself from bursting with my release.

"I'll be back, for more," she said running a finger over the tip of my cock, before finally stepping away.

By the gods! That had been one of the most sensual and arousing moments of my life. I couldn't wait for her return.

My mind played with images of us together, not really watching as she went to Aethan and had her moment with him. Her words with him were lost to me. I saw them kiss and my heart only swelled for my friend, confirming what my soul said was true: that the four of us belong with Annie.

But something else was swelling too and if I didn't have her now, I was going to explode.

She finished with Aethan, returned to the bed, and laid back, her legs inching open just a hint and her smile turning coy again. "Some time ago, you all promised to ravish me..."

I didn't need any more permission—

Except despite my near-to-bursting erection, I wasn't a small man and I didn't know if she'd be ready for me.

I knelt next to the bed and, sliding my hands up the insides of her thighs, I leaned down to help ensure she would be ready.

She drew in a sharp breath of pleasure as I brushed my lips against her folds, teased my tongue into her, then swept it up her opening and flicked the tip across her clit.

She was wet, and getting more so, and would be ready soon enough, and I guessed her anticipation to join with us had been as aching as mine to join with her.

I kissed and licked, adding my moisture to the mix and drawing soft sighs and making her hips start a slow rocking against my mouth.

"Oh, yes," she sighed, and I flicked my tongue against her clit over and over again, feeling it swell, then sucked on it hard and was rewarded with a deeper sigh of pleasure.

Gods I loved that sound, and I loved it even more coming from Annie.

Lifting my lips away, I slid two fingers into her to test if she was wet and relaxed enough for me. She was close, so I reached deep within her, curling my fingers up to find the magic spot that would heighten her pleasure. With my thumb on her clit, I rocked my hand back and forth, fingers pressing inside, thumb on the outside, working her up until her legs tensed, closing around my head a little and she groaned. Her muscles contracted around my fingers as she shuddered, and she released a loud, breathy moan, as her wetness rushed around my fingers and her body relaxed further.

Now she was ready.

I climbed onto the bed, sitting back on my heels, pulled her closer, and began a slow, teasing thrust into her fully aroused opening.

CHAPTER 8

ANNIE

I LET OUT A SERIES OF QUICK GASPS AS DEL PUSHED INTO me. He was big, but thanks to the man's exquisite work with his lips, tongue, and fingers I was more than ready for him. Still, just because I could accommodate his large cock, didn't mean I was prepared for the sensation of it slowly filling me. I felt every rigid inch, every bulging vein. It was a blissful agony as I waited for him to bury himself fully, but Del was going so... very... slowly.

I moaned and rolled my head to the side.

It was only then that I saw Aethan, standing at the foot of the bed, erect and ready, his expression pinched as he waited patiently.

My body warmed and tingled with its newly acquired connection to him. "You don't need to wait," I breathed. "There are many parts of me a man can love."

God, where had that come from?

I'd never have said anything like that a few weeks ago. I hadn't thought any part of me was particularly lovable. I knew men were drawn to my full breasts, but I figured once they saw the freckles covering my girls that would be a turn-off.

"Of course, my goddess." Aethan climbed onto the bed.

That was something else I'd never have imagined a few weeks ago. Not only were men calling me a goddess, but... I felt like one. I was worshiped and adored, but more than that, I now possessed more power than I'd ever imagined. I could feel all of their abilities thrumming through me, strength, light, speed, and water. It was amazing. Nearly as amazing as what Del was doing.

He finished his tantalizingly slow thrust, my legs falling wide to accommodate his body. He wasn't as long as Rion, nor as massive as Keph, but that didn't matter. He still felt amazing inside me.

Aethan crawled up the bed next to me, resting on one arm as he leaned down to kiss the oh-so-sensitive nipple of my right breast. His other hand reached out to cup my other breast, and began to massage it, working both of my nipples into tight, aching buds.

Oh, yes! This was just fine with me. To reward the man for his dedicated work, I reached down and wrapped my hand around his cock. He grunted. He must have taken that as a sign I wanted things a little rougher, and he raked his teeth over my nipple.

Oh, wow. His lips formed a seal and he sucked hard, his teeth running roughly over the area again. I cried out in pleasure, in part because of the sensation shooting straight to my core and because Del was finishing the slow withdrawal from his first thrust and I wanted him back, deep inside me again.

Del's next thrust was hard, fast, and surprising. I yelped again, and Aethan growled low as his whole body tensed. Crap. I'd squeezed his cock at Del's sudden thrust.

Except it didn't feel as if Aethan was upset, more like he was trying not to come. He trembled and sucked in sharp breaths and I was sure he *was* going to come, but somehow he managed to hold himself together. God, the man had an incredible control.

He moved his lips from my breast to my mouth, and kissed with a ferocious, urgent passion. It was far different than the deep, soft and lingering kiss we'd had when I'd claimed him. That had been precious and lasting, lips and tongues mingling in a long, sensual union. This was rough and fierce, and I returned the kiss in kind, tangling my hands in his red mohawk and holding him close.

After a wild, breathtaking moment, he jerked away, and his soft brown eyes were not-so-soft anymore. Fiery passion filled them and his chest heaved with deep, rapid breaths. "I need you."

I felt the same. I wanted him inside me and was about to pull that cock of his up to my lips, when Del said, "Aethan, move away."

The *satyr* looked down at the triton with fire and death in his eyes. He didn't want to move, didn't want to leave being so close to me.

"No," Aethan growled.

"Trust me," Del said with a smile and a wink, "you're going to like this."

Aethan frowned, confusion seeping into his passion, but he eased back as ordered.

I was a little confused as well. What was Del thinking?

He didn't say, but, fully inside me, he reached down, hands under my butt and back and lifted me. I did my fair share of planking, but never really thought I had the 'firm and solid' core of most of the girls at the gym. But with Keph's strength lingering in me, I lifted myself up, wrapping my arms around Del's neck to help support me. With a moan, I wrapped my legs around his hips and pulled myself closer to him, pushing him deeper inside me.

"What are you—" I tried to ask, but with his hands on my butt he had a lot of control and used it to grind me down into him for a moment, which drew more gasps, stopping whatever I was going to say.

He turned and shifted, swiveling around to lay back. I unwrapped my legs from him, straddling his hips, my full weight pressing down onto that amazing cock.

Del pulled me down, my breasts pressed against his wide hard chest. "How would you feel about both of us inside you at once?" he asked with a mischievous glint in those sea-green eyes. His blue-black hair splayed over my pillow.

Oh?

Aethan moved behind me, straddling Del's legs, and realization kicked in.

Oh!

Aethan pressed his cock against my other entrance, teasing around the sensitive area, letting me know what he intended while waiting for permission.

"Oh, yes!" I exclaimed. I'd never done anything like

that before, but I so desperately wanted both of them in me, and Aethan deserved a reward for his incredible patience. "Oh, yes. There's lube in the table beside the bed."

"Lube?" Aethan asked.

"It makes things slide better. I've heard you need it for—" My pulse skipped a beat in anticipation. "For that."

"Oh, like oil!" Aethan's eyes lit up and out of the corner of my eye I watched him open my night table drawer and pull out the lube—thankfully even if he wasn't familiar with tubes of lube, the container was the only thing in my nightstand that looked like it might hold a liquid.

He poured a liberal amount into his palm and pumped his hand up and down his length a few times, before drawing close again, his heavy, shuddering breath washing over my back.

This time, he grabbed my hips, pressing himself at my entrance again, then, pushed slowly past the tight ring of muscle, filling me with a seductive fiery sensation, pleasure mixed with a lick of pain.

He entered inch by inch, pacing himself and giving me time to adjust to him— to both of them filling me. His body trembled—

No. He wasn't trembling so much as... vibrating. The rapid micro-movements of his cock were like nothing I'd ever felt before, heightening my pleasure, twisting me tighter, and relaxing my muscles so he could fully sheath himself within me. And while I had a vibrator, I'd never used it there. God, I was an idiot for not even imagining that this might be something I'd love, because man, this was incredible!

He sank in all the way, his breath heavy, my breath and Del's heavy as well. Need thrummed through me. With my hands on Del's shoulders, I pushed myself up to arm's length and started to slowly rock my hips, unable to stay still.

Aethan slid his hands, also now vibrating in the same way—perhaps all of him was—from my hips, up my belly to my breasts. This was another sensitive area where I'd never thought to use a vibrator, but the way he gripped, pulsating as he was, nearly made me come. Certainly, I was on the verge now.

Shivering lips pressed against my shoulder and neck as he leaned forward. His whole body was vibrating. Oh, God!

Del's hands replaced Aethan's on my hips, urging me quicker in my rocking movement atop him. I knew he was close. I could feel his cock swelling inside me, his head pressed back into the sheets, his gorgeous long blue-black hair splayed around him, but I didn't want him to come yet.

On instinct, I used his water powers, reached into his body and clasped shut the flow of his release at the base of his cock.

He grunted, back lifting from the bed, gasping in—what looked like—exquisite, blissful pain.

I opened my mouth to apologize and release him, but his gaze locked with mine, desire burning in his eyes.

"Don't you dare release me," he said. "I want you to come first."

Gasping, I mentally held him on the precipice as Aethan pumped harder and harder into me, building me up.

I was ready, oh so ready, and a wave of ecstasy so powerful and encompassing I thought I might drown in it, crashed over me with a violent shudder. That was all Aethan needed to find his release and I let go of Del so he'd come at the same time.

The three of us cried out in a series of grunts, wordless screams, and low moans. Yet I got the best of the three of us. Feeling their twin release within me was the most powerful and bliss-inducing thing I'd ever felt and my orgasm simply kept going as the two men pulsed inside me.

Slowly they relaxed, spent, but I remained rigid and trembling in my climax, clamped onto each of their cocks, unwilling to let go.

Aethan began massaging my back, his hand no longer vibrating, just soft and relaxing, while Del messaged my front... which had a whole other, opposite reaction.

When I finally released them, Aethan sighed and withdrew, and I slowly lifted myself off Del and flopped onto my back in the bed, tired for the moment, but still buzzed, my body hypersensitive. And with the two men, one on either side of me now—a little cramped on my double-bed—caressing various parts of me, I was quickly trembling with renewed anticipation.

Aethan slowly slid his hand, vibrating yet again, down my body, and teased the insides of my thigh. That vibration ability of his, moving himself so incredibly quickly, was really quite the trick. Del, on his side, traced lazy fingers over my face, shoulders, arms, and breasts. Where he touched, he left lines of fiery pleasure whispering through my skin, and I finally couldn't take it anymore. The barest of touches was too much, I needed hard and firm. I grabbed his hand and pressed it to a breast.

"Harder," I whispered to him.

He gave a nod, his strong hands gripping and pressing on my flesh as he leaned down and kissed my shoulder. Here again, he began soft and tender. I fixed that quickly, reaching around his neck and head, to pull his lips to mine. I was quickly building to another peak, feeling feral, needing things rough.

My body shuddered as Aethan's pressing fingers brought me to a small climax. Except it wasn't a climax at all, just a ridge on my way to a much higher peak.

Del was all in now, hands and lips hard and demanding. He kissed his way down to where his hand was working on my breast and, as Aethan had earlier, nipped at my hypersensitive nipple. That elevated the wave of bliss I was riding, drawing a gasping, shuddering moan.

"Harder," I whispered again.

He grunted and bit me. I yelped as pleasure spiked hard in my core. Oh, yes! That was exactly what I wanted. A little pain, a whole lot of pleasure.

He plucked my peaked nipple, drawing another delicious spike of pain. Moaning, I arched my back, my body begging for more.

Oh yes, yes, yes.

I'd never wanted anything like this before, never been

interested in pain adding to pleasure, but in this instant, it was exactly what I wanted.

Aethan moved, settling on the bed between my legs, resting my calves on his shoulders. He cupped his hands under my butt to raise my hips, pulling me close. With his shivering cock aligned with my opening, he stared down at me, his gaze filled with breathtaking desire and love.

Never before had I felt so wonderful, powerful, and confident with my legs up in the air. Then Aethan pushed into my more-than-ready opening, his vibrating cock sliding against my uber-sensitive channel, making me nearly come with just a single thrust. Shuddering again, I found a new peak and rode that, sensing that I hadn't yet reached the top.

CHAPTER 9

AETHAN

I COULD SEE THE EFFECT I WAS HAVING ON ANNIE. THE WAY her body trembled, her muscles contracting on the verge of release as my vibrating cock found every sensitive inch of her.

She groaned, the sound muffled against Del's mouth, the man kissing her with a ferocity I didn't realize he was capable of.

It took everything I had not to give in and start thrusting with a matching wildness. But this wasn't about me. It was about Annie and her pleasure, and I shifted her hips a little until she moaned low, bucking in my hands, telling me I'd hit the right spot.

Then I slowly withdrew and pushed back in, hitting the spot again. She clung to Del's head, her fingers tangled in his hair, their lips battling, her breath quick, her gorgeous breasts heaving with each rapid breath.

Another withdrawal and push, this time faster, and her hips rose to meet me, sending a tremor through me that I shoved aside.

I wouldn't come before her. I. Would. Not. It was actually astounding that I was ready to come again so soon after the first time, but I could feel my balls tightening, on the verge of another release.

I shifted forward a little, resting her hips on the top of my thighs, and swept my vibrating hands over her belly, sending one up toward those incredible breasts and the other to her mound, where I messaged her clit with my thumb.

Her hips jerked again.

"Oh, God yes. Please, Aethan, please," she begged, her voice filled with undeniable pleasure.

It astounded me and filled me with such awe. I'd never felt this confident with a woman before or this in control and powerful

But then, no woman had claimed me like Annie had.

That kiss, the moment of our bonding, had been the most inspirational, astounding kiss of my entire life. I'd felt the bond form, my soul locked with hers as our lips had played and roamed. But the true joy had come from simply knowing that she'd wanted to claim me.

Me.

Aethan, the sexual outcast, the uncontrolled 'lusty' *satyr*.

Just knowing that had been enough. Then she *had* claimed me, the magic of our bonding flooding me with strength and power. It was more than I could have ever expected. And from that had come this newfound confidence and control in my love-making.

Even now, I was exceptionally aroused, and seeing Annie's multiple orgasms and knowing I was causing that was enough to make me burst. But I wouldn't. I'd keep my release back, giving Annie so many orgasms she melted into a pool of quivering flesh before I gave myself any kind of release.

And I was well on my way to that goal.

She seemed to have no control over her hips now, the way they were writhing from my ministrations, and she mewled and begged into Del's mouth, no longer kissing him, just holding on for dear life.

"Enough!" she gasped, pushing Del aside and sliding her legs off my shoulders, to sit up. She grabbed my head and— riding so high upon me—pressed my face into the softness of her breasts and ground down on me. "Come, damn you!"

Her hips thrust down hard, and she screamed, her whole body tensing with her release.

I let myself go in that instant as well, my mouth pressed to the top of one of her breasts.

She stayed there for some time, her body jerking with pleasure, her breath hard and fast, as my own release crashed through me.

"Holy fucking-fuck," she gasped. "With guys like you around, I might never leave my bedroom again!" She kissed the top of my head then leaned back a little, which meant my face was no longer pressed into her bosom, giving me a perfect view of her amazing speckled breasts. It was hard to take my eyes off them, but I managed to drag my gaze away and look up at her.

"I thought nothing would beat that first round, with both of you inside me—" She squirmed as if just the thought turned her on again. "But gods! This second time was entirely different and just as amazing!" She squirmed again, pulling herself up a little to rub her breasts against my chest, her soft skin sending tingles rushing through me. If she squirmed much more, I'd be ready for a third round in no time.

But alas, she moved off me and flopped down on the bed. "I don't know how, but I'm both exhausted and more alive and energized than I've ever been before. I feel like I could take on the world."

"I believe," Del said with a satisfied grin, "that was the point."

I'd never shared a woman before, but with him it seemed almost natural. We were close enough as friends that it hadn't been awkward. Instead it had been— Well, it had been the best sex I'd had in my entire life. I, too, felt powerful and ready to take on the world—and also just a little exhausted.

"Let's see if the others are awake. I think it's time to make some plans," Annie said sliding over to the edge of the bed. She tried to stand but couldn't, sitting back down on the bed heavily, laughing.

"My legs don't work," she giggled. "You two have fucked me so hard my legs don't work." She turned back to us. "I guess one of you will have to carry me into the other room."

With my super-speed, I was up and beside her, standing next to the bed with my hand extended in an instant.

Annie started at my sudden arrival next to her. "I'm going to have to get used to that," she murmured. "Hand me that robe." She pointed behind me to the heavy, fuzzy garment on the floor.

I did as asked, and she put it on while sitting, then smiled up at me. "Okay, now I'm ready, let's go."

I rushed her first to the bathroom where we cleaned up a bit, then into her common area and set her in a chair at her dining table. Thankfully, unlike the first time I'd used my speed with her in my arms, she wasn't sick. Instead she was giggling again.

"I think now that I have access to your ability, I'm good with being whisked around like that."

Well that was good, because I wanted to whisk her anywhere and everywhere.

"Any time," I said with a bow.

"You sure made a lot of noise in there," Rion said, sitting up on the couch. "Could hardly get a wink of sleep out here." Yet he was smiling and looked refreshed enough.

Del strode out of Annie's bathroom, also cleaned up, and joined Rion on the couch, while Keph sat up from his spot on the floor, but stayed where he was.

"Good," Annie said. "We're all ready. Time to get down to business."

CHAPTER 10

ANNIE

"Well... fuck," I hissed, muting the TV.

With the *naiad*'s duplicates having been out in the world while I'd been healing everyone in the convention center—yeah... I'd done that... wow!—I'd wondered if there'd been anything on the news about a spreading disease. And it hadn't been good news.

I'd forgotten about Disease Man. I mean I hadn't really forgotten about him, I just hadn't thought about the implications of him also being able to spread the disease. He'd been sent to the hospital because Keph had seriously hurt him in his world, and I'd assumed when the *naiad* had infected the paramedics instead of him that he hadn't kept his powers in this world.

Except Mercy Hospital was reporting a massive outbreak of a nasty disease, one with black spots and terrible death, and it was looking like he—just like I had —had kept his powers. The disease wouldn't have spread as rapidly or killed as quickly if it had only come from those two paramedics.

"Fuck, fuck, fuck."

The guys sat around me, Aethan to my left, Rion on my right, while Del leaned on the back of the couch behind me and Keph sat on the floor by my feet. They were tense. I could feel it even without looking at them.

"He's kept his powers too, it seems," Rion said.

"Yeah, and now I have a lot more people to heal." I wasn't happy about that at all. From the soaring heights of magnificent sex... to that. It made a girl want to gather up her little harem and go get her brains fucked out all over again... preferably some place warm and tropical.

But that silly line from that movie kept repeating in my head. It was my responsibility to help because I could. In fact, with my healing magic I was uniquely suited to do so.

"And we need to deal with this fucker," I said, standing. "I won't let him infect any more—"

"Ah... Annie?" Aethan said.

I looked at him. He pointed at the TV. The story had turned from the outbreak to a murder at the same hospital and was showing a picture of the man who'd been murdered.

"That's him," Aethan said softly. "That's the man who spread the disease."

I blinked. I hadn't actually seen Disease Man so I had no idea what he looked like.

"Wait, what?" I'd automatically assumed the murder victim had been killed by Disease Man for getting in his way as he'd tried to leave the hospital or something, but if the victim was the man spreading the disease...

My head spun. This didn't make any sense... and yet...

my words to Del from earlier came back to me: Disease Man is still out there and I can't shake the feeling that he's not the only one like me who can travel between worlds.

I don't know how I knew that, but I was sure that Disease Man hadn't been killed by any normal person. In fact, I was certain it had been someone special like him and me.

But fuck! I didn't know what that meant.

I slumped back onto the couch.

"Annie?" Keph asked, concerned. "What is it?"

Aethan shifted closer, while Rion laid a hand on my thigh and Del placed his on my shoulder. Keph turned, kneeling before me and looked at me—our eyes were level when he sat like that. His gaze was filled with love and certainty, but it was clear he was still worried. They all were. But with just a shift of their body language and a determined look in their eyes, they were telling me that they had my back, whatever I chose to do.

I looked at each of them in turn.

"How did I get so lucky?" I hadn't really meant to say that out loud. But hearing my voice say those words, and seeing the concerned looks of the men around me, gorgeous, powerful men who loved me... my emotions broke and with a smile that trembled with a sad mix of joy and gratitude, a tear traced down my cheek.

"You were just you," Rion said softly.

Those were the exact right words I needed to hear.

I wiped away that tear and drew myself up. "Well boys, it seems we have a mystery to solve and some people to heal. Get dressed. We're going out again."

They all dispersed at my words to find their discarded clothes. I pulled out my phone to call Janice from the FBI. I wasn't sure what I was going to say if she asked me about the *naiad*—and a part of me hoped she wouldn't say anything—but I doubted that. She knew we'd had one of the *triplets* in custody and it was her job to apprehend those responsible for this bio-terrorist attack.

Except there wasn't anyone else who might be able to help us. Janice already knew that I, and the people we were after, had powers.

I pulled up her text and was about to dial her number when my phone rang. I was so surprised I dropped it onto my lap.

Picking it up again, I looked at the name: Diane Jenkins.

Work.

Fuck!

What day was it? I had no clue. I'd been healing the convention center for what felt like a week, but I knew it hadn't been that long. Still, it had been longer than a weekend from when I'd first gone back to find the guys infected with the terrible disease. Which meant it was sometime in the work week and I hadn't gone in to work at all.

I answered. At least it was Diane and not my boss.

"Where the fuck are you?" she snapped. "I've been holding down the fort here, but Jake is starting to get antsy. I've told him your bad flu acted up again, but I don't think he believes me anymore. If you want to keep this job, you need to get in here!"

Jake was my boss. The trouble was, I didn't have time

for my mundane job anymore. I had a more important job to do.

"Oh God, thank you Diane, but... I can't. And I can't explain why either. Trust me, you won't believe me and neither will Jake. I'm sorry." Time to make a decision. One I didn't like at all. "I'm sorry Diane, but... I think I need to quit. I'll tell Jake in person... well, I'll call him. My life has just been turned upside down these last few weeks and..." And I had other priorities now. Like saving a city from the outbreak of a nasty disease. Then finding out who else was like me and what they wanted. But I couldn't tell her any of that. "And... yeah, sorry."

"Annie, I hope you're okay," she said, sounding concerned and not upset or angry like I expected. "It won't be the same here without you. I'll miss you. We really need to have a coffee some time and you can tell me all about the things no one will believe."

"I will," I said, lying. Not that I didn't want to have coffee with her. I enjoyed her company. But because I wasn't sure where I'd be when all of this was said and done.

We hung up and I quickly dialed my boss. He answered with a harsh, "Annie, where have you been? Are you okay?"

"I am, and I can't explain all the details. But a lot has come up in my life and I can't keep this job anymore. I'm sorry. You've been good to me, and I wish I could stay on until you found someone else, but I just can't. Sorry."

He harrumphed. "I figured it might be something like that. Sad to lose you. Take care." And he hung up. He'd had that 'I'm not angry, I'm disappointed' tone of voice, which was always worse than just being angry, but there wasn't anything I could do about that.

I clenched my jaw for a long moment, wondering how in the hell I was going to pay my rent then quickly dialed Janice before the pressure of the responsibility and panic over the situation took over. I needed to just keep moving, keep focusing on what was important, and that was stopping an 'evil someone' with powers like me.

Janice didn't sound surprised to hear from me—and she didn't sound angry that I'd just up and left the convention center without handing over the *naiad*. Of course maybe she had more important things to worry about, like a rapidly spreading plague.

"Oh, thank God," Janice said. "Have you heard about the hospital?"

"Just saw it on TV, yeah. I'm on my way there."

"I'll send a car. It can get you here faster," she replied.

"A van would be better. With really good rear suspension. I have big friends."

She chuckled. "Yeah, I remember. Lucky you. Car'll be there in five. I'll meet you out front when you get here."

And that was it.

Hunh. Maybe I worked for the FBI now. I'd have to ask Janice if I could get paid to do this healing stuff.

Me. Working for the FBI. Now there was something I'd never expected to think about.

I bet they had an amazing health plan—

The thought made me snort.

I didn't need to have a health plan anymore. I *was* my health plan.

The guys were ready well before I was. Though their suits were all looking a little wrinkled and rough and Rion had lost both his shirt and jacket—

And shit, that was the suit I'd borrowed from Margie for my brother's wedding... which also reminded me that I'd have to explain the guys to my brother and family at some point.

Which would be... awkward, to say the least.

And really, it could wait. It wasn't a priority.

Thankfully I still had the secondhand long-sleeved T-shirt I'd originally bought him when I'd first bought them clothes. It didn't fit the FBI vibe of the others, but it was black and at least matched his pants. That and Keph didn't exactly fit the FBI vibe, either. There hadn't been a suit jacket big enough for him and he'd ripped out the sleeves of his dress shirt.

I had the world's quickest shower and dressed in comfortable slacks and a merino wool pull-over shirt I loved. It was warm, but also form fitting. I was comfortable and looked hot. Odd... I wouldn't have used that word before. I would have said I looked "good", but not "hot." Perhaps having four hot guys who'd devoted their lives to me had changed how I saw myself, but I didn't have a lot of time to mull it over before the car arrived.

It was your standard black government SUV, and it didn't completely give way when Keph got in. So that was good. Although the driver did seem a bit shaken at how the car rocked as Keph settled into his seat.

I sat up front next to the driver and smiled. "He's big boned."

God! That brought up thoughts of his 'bone' which

made me giggle. The man looked at me strangely, and I snapped my mouth shut, swallowing my laughter. Government workers shouldn't giggle. But then I thought of all of the guys' 'bones' and how they were all commando under those suits. That was just a little too sexy a thought for being on my way to heal hundreds of people and I pressed my legs together and thought of diseases. Yeah, that dried me up real quick.

The car had a hidden set of flashing lights and a siren, so, we blasted through traffic and were at the hospital in record time.

All the entrances to the hospital had heavy plastic quarantine entrances set up in front of the actual entrances with men standing guard from preventing anyone from entering or exiting the building.

Janice stood out front in a black coat, huddled against the strong wind coming off the lake. Flurries blasted sideways around us as the guys and I went over to meet her. When this was all over, I was going to join the guys in their world for a while. I deserved a vacation... with four sexy cabana boys serving my every whim. Oh yeah, that was happening.

For now, though...

"What do we know?" I asked as we got close.

She led us to a temporary structure a couple dozen feet away from the hospital. The temporary structure wasn't what I'd call comfortable. Even though there were heaters blasting, it was still a bit chilly. At least it was out of the wind. Perhaps it hadn't been here long enough for those heaters to do their job. Inside FBI agents and doctors bustled about and consulted with people wearing CDC jackets.

Perhaps someone at the CDC had actually listened to my warning call.

Janice stopped at a small table near the back with piles of papers scattered on it. "The numbers we're getting at the moment are roughly five hundred infected, with over a dozen fatalities so far and a few more on the brink." She looked up. "Are you recovered now? It's only been about a day since I saw you last." She squinted at me. "You certainly look recovered. In fact, you look great. God—!" Her mouth quirked. "Perhaps I should be saying *goddess*?"

"I'm feeling well enough to tackle this. Five hundred doesn't seem like that many."

"Really?" Janice asked, her eyes widening. "It seems like a whole lot to me. And they're far more infected here than they were at the convention center."

"Right, good point," I replied. "That will take more out of me, but I still think I can do it." I turned to Keph. "Ready to help me with some strength?"

He nodded, though he didn't look as refreshed as I felt after a day away from this slogging work.

"You can have strength from all of us," Aethan said. "I know we're not as strong as Keph is, but we can help."

I held out my hand to him and Keph. "Then help you shall, let's do this."

"Here? Now?" Janice said. "I thought you had to touch the person."

Oh, right... and yet...

That had been true yesterday, but I hadn't possessed Del's powers over water. I hadn't even realized it, but I was sensing all of those 'bodies' of water around me. And even at a distance, in the hospital, I felt the various people in there. More than that, combined with my own healing ability and knowledge of this disease, I knew who was infected and who wasn't. I could heal them from where I was. It would take more effort, but it would save time and with lives on the line, that was what was most important right now.

"Yes, here."

"You continue to amaze me," Janice whispered in awe.

"I continue to amaze myself," I mumbled, then I closed my eyes and reached out. I sought the most infected first, some with the very last of their lives ebbing from them. Those I healed first. There were perhaps twenty in such need, and another fifty or so not far off.

Aethan gasped, releasing my hand and staggering back. Oops, I must have drawn too much from him.

"Sorry," I said, returning to myself. I looked over at him. He was pale, his eyes wide.

"I'm fine," he gasped, clearly not fine. But I knew he'd recover without any additional healing from me, he just needed time.

Rion stepped in to replace him, taking my hand.

"You sure?" I asked.

He nodded.

"Here we go again." I felt back to those in the hospital. Now, with the dire cases taken care of, I could take a bit more time. And time it took. Somewhere along the line Rion let go and Del stepped in.

I finished with those at the hospital and still had

power to spare, though I was exhausted and felt Del and Keph were too, but still... There were people out in the city who could be spreading the disease. I needed to heal everyone, and I might as well do it now before there were twice as many infected.

So I reached out past the hospital, growing my awareness of 'infected-water' to the entire city. It strained my new-found powers with water to do so, but I felt I had a good enough radius to hopefully catch everyone now. I pushed healing out to the hundreds— No thousands of infected bodies. Luckily, most of the infections were mild and easy to heal.

Del fell away. Even Keph released me and—as if through distant ears—I'd heard a thud and a shake of the earth. My pulse stuttered for a moment and I prayed he was well, but I had to finish what I started or everything I'd done so far would have been a waste.

Time expanded, drawn out, as I moved from body to body, water to water, healing... so very many.

Then... it was done! The city was cleansed.

I drew in a long breath, my head spinning, and opened my eyes to find the guys resting around me and myself sitting in a chair that hadn't been near me before.

"I'm done," I said, though it came out as a croak, my voice hoarse.

It was dark outside. At some point the sun had set and I hadn't noticed.

Janice looked over from some papers she was reviewing. "You've healed the entire hospital?"

"I've healed the entire city."

Her jaw dropped and her eyes flashed wide. Then her

expression turned serious. "Was that worth it? We still haven't found the final triplet. She could still be out there infecting people. The one we had in custody died. Or at least we think she died, then she disappeared, but we never found the last one." She glanced around the tent then drew closer. "And you never handed over the one you caught."

Crap. I knew it would happen, but I'd been seriously hoping she'd have forgotten about that.

My pulse tried to pick up with fear that she was going to arrest me and my guys, but I was just too exhausted.

"We've taken care of the one we caught and her... sister," I said, praying she'd accept that and not force me to outright lie to her. Then I realized that 'take care of' could mean we'd killed her. "She's— They're not dead, but they won't cause any more trouble. Our prisons wouldn't really be able to hold her and—"

"And the fewer people who know, the better," Janice said with a tight nod. "I'm not sure how I'm going to explain any of this to my boss. I'm not even sure I completely get what's going on, but we owe you and I'd rather not make trouble for a goddess."

I released the breath I hadn't realized I'd been holding. "Thank you."

"I'll let people know the hospital and the city are disease free. They'll want to do their own verification of course, but..." Janice shook her head as if she still couldn't believe I'd just healed the entire city and headed to the front of the tent to speak to two women standing over another table.

I slumped in my chair, exhausted.

"How're you guys doing?" I asked.

Keph was out cold and snoring, but I got nods from the others. Good.

"I can't believe you did that," Aethan said, his voice filled with awe. He looked the most recovered out of all of them. "You exhausted us all, even Keph and then kept going for hours!"

"That's me," I said, eyes drooping, exhaustion pulling at me. "Annie Chambers, Goddess extraordinaire!" Then I fell into a black pit of unconsciousness.

CHAPTER 11

KEPHAS

I BLINKED MY EYES OPEN. THE HARSH LIGHT OF ONE OF THE miracle lanterns of Annie's world pierced my eyes, and I sat up so I wouldn't be looking directly at it.

We were still in the strange tent outside the hospital and I was still tired and drained, but I had no idea how much time had passed. I'd given Annie everything I could, then I'd simply sat down, fell back, and slept on the spot. When you're used to sleeping on stone, every-where was comfortable.

"Look who's up," Del said with a nod in my direction. "I didn't think we'd see you for a while."

"I'm tougher than *you* look." It was a joke, but it came out dry and harsher than I wanted.

Del looked a bit offended at first, then shrugged and nodded. "Well... yeah, you are."

Annie was asleep, draped in a chair, her legs splayed out in front of her, not looking comfortable at all.

"We should lay her down," I said.

The other guys all looked over and then looked to

each other. "Why didn't any of us think of that?" Rion asked.

"We're all tired," Del said, gently picking Annie up and moving her to a small bed, which looked to be little more than fabric pulled taut over a metal frame.

Then we all simply stared at her for a long moment.

I didn't know what the others were thinking so I figured I might as well say my thoughts. "She's truly amazing."

The other three nodded solemnly.

"She kept going long after you collapsed," Aethan said. "I didn't think..." He shook his head. "Yes, amazing." I could sense his awe and wonder... and love. I felt it from all of them.

"So... is this our life now?" Rion asked.

It was the same question I'd been thinking, and from Del's grunt and Aethan's nod, I could tell they'd been thinking the same thing. We'd all bonded with Annie, dedicating our lives to hers, but... I didn't think any of us had truly thought about what that would mean for us.

"It is," Del said softly. "And speaking of our lives, there's something I need to tell you all."

"You're the 'great prince' of Galniosia you're always talking about?" Aethan said. It was a question, but he already knew the answer.

Del's eyes widened with surprise and it was Aethan's turn to grunt.

"Yeah, we know," he said. "Figured it out a long time ago."

I hadn't figured it out, but then I wasn't as quick witted as Aethan was. But he had told me the last time our group had met, so I wasn't surprised by the announcement.

"You do? You did?" Del asked.

We all nodded.

"But... you let me go on..." Del, frowned, his expression turning a little pained. "I must have looked like such a fool."

"Yeah, but we love you anyway." Aethan punched him lightly on the shoulder and chuckled and Del released a heavy sigh.

"Well anyway, I considered what it would mean to devote myself to Annie and I'm ready to give up my title. I'd give up anything for her." I could see the truth of that in his blue-green eyes, his devotion and dedication the same as mine.

"I'll be giving up my position as well," Rion said, sounding like he was just making the decision as he spoke. "I can't be in the sky navy of my people and here with Annie. I can't have divided loyalties, and frankly, I didn't want the promotion I was about to get anyway. This life will be much... simpler. Though I suspect it won't always be easy. Like today."

That was true.

And I was glad for Rion. He'd seemed so torn when he'd told us about his promotion. He hadn't talked much about his life back in the Phyllidian Forest, except to say it hadn't been easy. Yet, I got the sense there was far more behind those few words. I got the sense he felt driven to prove himself, but to who or why I didn't know, and I'd never asked. Yet, now that he'd given his life over to Annie, he seemed much happier.

"I have little to leave behind," I said. "I have no title or position. The only reason I was selected as emissary was because I had an interest to see the rest of the world, which is an anomaly among my people." Warm contentment seeped into me, my words making me feel steady and certain. This was where I belonged and who I belonged with. "I, too, have accepted this new life. Even if I'm going to spend most of it sitting, it seems. But then again, that's nothing new. I've had to do that everywhere outside the stone halls of my people."

We all looked at Aethan.

He shrugged. "I have little to give up. I wasn't anyone important and most of my people were glad to have me go off and be our emissary. I'm like you Keph, I just wanted to see other places. I guess I'm doing that by Annie's side now." But there was far more behind his casual words. I sensed his new-found confidence and inner-strength and was glad he'd found that.

"Then we're in accord?" Del asked. "All together? All for Annie?"

We all nodded.

"So..." Rion cleared his throat, his expression turning uncomfortable. "Are we all set on... sharing her?"

"I don't see any issues with it," Del said. "Aethan and I were together with her and it was..." His brow furrowed. "Well, if you'd told me before all this that I'd be sharing a woman in bed with another man, I'd have scoffed at you. That idea didn't appeal to me at all, but..." A soft, silly grin tugged at his lips. "With Annie, it's different. I want her to have everything, the highest heights of joy, and if that means another man is with her when I am, I can accept that." He shrugged, his smile growing. "And frankly, you're all like brothers to me. There's no one I'd rather share her with."

"Exactly," Aethan said. "We've all dedicated ourselves to her, we're all hers, and that brings us even closer now. I think we also need to be dedicated to each other, and to our mutual... worship of our shared goddess."

Rion nodded and glanced at me. There was a hunger in his eyes, but I knew it wasn't for me, he was remembering something, and I think I knew what.

"When Annie was bonding with Keph, I found that incredibly—" He drew in a sharp breath. "I think this could work. We're not so much sharing as we're all dedicated to making her happy any way we can."

I nodded. "Agreed." Looking around at this odd structure of canvas and metal, I shook my head. "Even if that means living in her world, strange as it is."

"I would like to learn to operate one of those *cars*!" Aethan said excited.

"I would like to get back to some water once this is all over... with all of you, and Annie of course," Del's said wistfully.

"And I to the skies," Rion added. "I fear that I may need to find some secluded place for that in this world."

I didn't really have a grand desire. Well I guess I did. I just wanted to be able to stand up inside and not break anything. But that was unlikely in most places I went, not just here in Annie's world.

"I don't know about the rest of you, but I'm looking forward to what comes next," Aethan said, which was obvious from his pent-up energy.

"Careful, you might just get something you didn't want at all," I advised.

His gaze darted out the opening to the hospital and he grimaced. "I suppose."

Annie stirred and we all turned to her, but she didn't wake, just adjusted herself on the small bed.

When Del turned back to the group, he, too, was frowning. "What if the old gods were like her? From her world?"

"You mean the ancient gods?" Aethan asked. "I guess that could be possible. If they had powers because they weren't from our world, *and* also acquired power from others like Annie has acquired ours, they'd certainly seem like gods to a more primitive culture than ours."

"Look around you, Aethan." Rion motioned to the tent we were in. "Our world, our culture is more primitive compared to this."

"I know, but I meant... *more* primitive. And we're not the only ones who think Annie is kin to gods. That other woman seems to believe it as well. So even in this advanced culture people are willing to believe someone with such powers is... god-like. Imagine what people thousands of years ago would have thought?"

Rion nodded. "True." He cocked his head. "But then, why weren't there more like Annie in the intervening times? What made the old gods disappear and why haven't there been others since?"

That was indeed a good question.

"Perhaps the portals, the ways to cross over from one world to another were somehow destroyed or limited?" I suggested. "If no one could find them then...?" I shrugged.

"That's very possible," Del said. "It seems likely. It would take just the right person to come in contact with just the right place."

Everyone nodded.

"If it is indeed that hard to cross over, then..." I looked over at Annie's slumbering form, my heart filled with desire and love for her. "What happened to us with Annie must have been fate."

CHAPTER 12

ANNIE

I woke feeling refreshed and sat up, swinging my leg over the side of the army cot that was tucked against the wall of the shelter outside the hospital. My guys were all close and looked over at me, their expressions warm and relaxed. There was something different about them, something... united?

"How long was I out?" I asked.

"Pretty much a full day," Aethan said with a soft smile.

Before I could ask about it, Janice came over.

"Good you're up. We've done a sweep of the hospital and everyone has been cured. They're calling it a miracle. Even though I know it was you, I still think it's a miracle." She shook her head. "If there's ever anything I can do for you, just let me know."

I grinned. "Actually, do you think I could be hired on as a contractor or something? All this running off to heal people in the middle of the day means I've lost my job."

"I don't know why it surprises me that you had a normal job. I'm assuming it *was* a normal job?"

"Yeah, admin guru at a software company. Then this whole god thing sort of got in the way."

"I bet," she said. "I'll see what I can do. I have no clue what I'd put down as your skill-set, but I'll figure something out. Maybe Immunologist? Anyway, thank you for everything. The car is ready to take you back to your place whenever you're ready." She nodded, then hurried off on other business.

So, perhaps I *could* get a job with the FBI. That would be... interesting.

I turned to the guys. "Shall we go?"

They nodded and stood with me. As we left, they formed up around me in a protective square. It was done without words, as if on instinct, and it made me shiver just a little with the precision and decisiveness, knowing this was all for me.

The large black SUV was parked at the side of the road, the driver outside. He nodded to us as we got near, but what drew my eye was the sleek white limousine parked a few feet in front of the SUV. A large man stood next to it as well, and as we drew close, he called out, "Annie Chambers?"

I stopped and all the guys tensed, ready for danger. Again, I got a thrill at the intense sense of protection and well-being I felt with the guys around.

"It's okay guys," I whispered. I didn't know if it was okay at all, but I felt reassured with them close by.

"Yes?" I called out to the man.

He motioned to the rear door of the limousine. "My employer would like a word with you."

A sense of foreboding whispered down my spine and

I fought a shudder. If this were a movie, it would mean I was about to speak with a benefactor or a baddie, and the benefactor was the least likely of the two options.

Except... I was curious. I'd been wondering if there was more going on and I had a sense this was the only way to find out.

"Sure." I headed for the limousine and without needing to tell the guys, they headed with me.

"I don't like this," Del muttered as the others made noises of agreement.

I was about to call to the driver of the SUV and tell him he wouldn't be needed when the man next to the limo called back, "Just you, not the men."

My heart froze.

Yeah, this wasn't going to be a warm and fuzzy meeting. Instantly I was on alert. I liked having the guys around me. It made me feel whole, loved, protected, and warm.

"Not going to happen," Rion said.

The limo driver shrugged. "If you want to find out what's going on, you'll come, alone," he replied to me.

And damn it. I *did* want to know what was happening. With Disease Man dead, I was pretty sure there was someone else with powers out there, and I couldn't risk that they weren't behind trying to infect the world.

Well, fuck.

"Annie, you can't go with them. I have a bad fee—" Del said, but I turned to him, cutting him off.

"Listen." I lowered my voice and spoke quickly. "Whoever this is might be behind the plot to infect everyone. Just because Disease Man is dead and we've healed everyone, doesn't necessarily mean this mess is over. We need more information and this is the only way to get it. Tell the SUV driver to follow us and that if he loses us, you'll tear off his head. Sound reasonable? That way you'll always be nearby."

They frowned at me, their expressions clear that they didn't like my plan and needed more. Frankly I wanted more assurance as well, but there wasn't much else we could do.

"Del, take out the phone I gave you." He did. "Turn it on."

I did the same with mine. The guys were huddled close, with Keph on the side facing the limo, and I was fairly certain no one would see me playing with my phone.

I quickly called the other phone then shoved my phone back into my pocket. "Leave your phone on. You'll be able to hear what's happening with me. If things go bad, have the driver ram the limo and stop us."

From their expressions, the guys still didn't like the plan, but this option seemed acceptable.

"Be careful," Aethan whispered.

"Always," I said, and flashed him a grin—though I wasn't feeling nearly as cocky as that grin let on.

The guys broke away from me, and moved toward the SUV. Suddenly I felt exposed and vulnerable... and normal. I knew that wasn't the case, that I still had powers. But I'd felt safe with the guys close.

The large man opened the limo door, and I slipped inside and sat on the rear seat of the large back passenger area.

I wasn't sure what I'd expected, but the immaculately attired and stunningly gorgeous woman sitting on the rear-facing seat at the front wasn't it. Her face was lean, but her lips were full. Large silver-blue eyes peered out from under perfectly tended lashes and brows and raven black hair framed her face, falling to her shoulders in lustrous waves.

There was no one else in the vehicle and I felt a bit better with it being just her and I, especially with all of the guy's powers tingling within me. I could be over to her in an instant with super speed, or blind her with Rion's light and be out of the car just as fast.

"So, who are you?" I asked as the driver closed the door, sealing me in with her.

The woman smiled, but it wasn't a friendly smile. Something about the predatory nature behind her eyes made the smile more like that of a tiger about to have lunch, and I was the lunch.

"Annie Chambers, I—"

"No, that's me, who are *you*?" I couldn't help the jab. It might not have been the smartest choice, but I couldn't help myself.

She blinked. "Impertinent, aren't we?"

"Just curious. You're the one who invited me in. Thought you should at least introduce yourself."

The driver got back into the driver's seat, started the car, and pulled away from the hospital.

"To the rest of the world I'm June Olympios," the woman said. "But you can call me by my real name. Hera."

One of the guys—Aethan, I think—swore so loud I could hear it faintly from the phone in my pocket.

June... or Hera, cocked her head to one side as if listening. She looked at me... then directly at my pocket.

"Do we have others listening in?" she asked, her tone darkening with annoyance, before raising a delicately sculpted eyebrow. "I suppose I can understand the precaution. But understand this, Annie, I'm not here to hurt you. I don't want to be your enemy. I want us to be friends."

Hera... That was Greek. My mind spun back to my one college class on mythology. Hera was the queen of the gods? Married to Zeus? I didn't know much more than that. It certainly wasn't a common name these days.

Also, I'd barely heard Aethan's voice over my phone and she was ten feet away. How had she heard?

Of course!

I'd already guessed there was someone else with powers involved in this, so I shouldn't have been surprised. The bigger question was: how much power did she have and was she the big boss or another henchman like Disease Guy? Also, was she on my side and not involved in trying to spread the plague—

No. From that evil look in her eyes, I doubted she was one of the good guys.

And I wouldn't really know anything unless I asked.

Well, she wanted to be friends... *Let's see how friendly she wants to be.*

"Your man said you'd explain what's going on. While you're at it, you can also tell me how you heard my phone from over there and... well if you want to be friends so

bad, you might as well tell me everything about yourself."
I sat back, hoping I looked over confident and had made
her think that I hadn't already figured out she had
powers. Hopefully if she thought I was stupid she'd tell
me more.

"That's fair." She leaned back as well, at ease,
mirroring or mocking my position. "My story begins
around three thousand years ago."

I tried not to gape.

Three *thousand* years? I hadn't expected that.

"You look good for your age," I said, hoping I sounded
calm and not completely shocked.

"I do, don't I?" She smiled, that same predatory smile.
Perhaps it was her only smile. "If you know anything
about Greek mythology, then you'll know the name
Hera."

"Queen of the gods?"

"Indeed, yes."

"And that was you?"

"It was."

Holy fuck. Three thousand years! "Your powers— You
— How—" I stammered all attempts to play it cool
vanishing.

I didn't know how that was possible. Could her magic
— could *my* magic let me live that long?

She chuckled at me as I opened my mouth and closed
it again.

"I was the first," she said, "But I was foolish enough to
share the knowledge with my friends. They too became
known as gods. Zeus, Athena, Ares, Poseidon, Demeter,
and so on."

The first? I couldn't help my eyes going a little wide at that. "Really?" I tried to sound interested and not stunned and knew I was failing miserably.

"I assume the four men with you are from Eytheron, the other world?"

She knew the name of the other world? That was a first. I wasn't even sure if the guys knew its name. I also didn't know how much to give away and hoped a simple: "Yes," wouldn't be too much information.

She nodded. "In my time, our two worlds were closer, the gateways much more numerous. Their kind came and went from our world and ours from theirs. Yet I was the first to forge a bond with one of them. And as you've done, I followed that up with others. I shared the bonding ability with my friends and as they gained powers, they rose to rule over our small corner of the world."

Of course they did. Because it couldn't have been kind, benevolent people who gained superpowers... and even if they had been kind, would they have eventually taken over? Would I? I was bulletproof thanks to Keph. It would take more than just a cop or FBI agent with a gun to stop me if I wanted to take over Chicago or even the world.

"As I'm sure you've discovered, you take their powers and keep your own. That was always how the bonds were meant to work, granting us greater powers and taking them from their kind."

"Taking?" I'd felt like it was more along the lines of borrowing. The way Hera spoke of it, it sounded like she could take their powers completely away from them.

"Little at first, but ultimately, yes, you can completely take their powers from them. That's how I've come to be who I am, with no others around me to hinder my progress. I was a goddess after all. I took what I needed or wanted and others... accepted it," she said casually.

Too casually. I could almost feel the frosted-mist rolling off her. This queen was made of ice.

"I have powers of immortality, hence why I've stayed so young, and you saw my enhanced senses at work a moment ago. I have other powers as well, but a woman needs her secrets. I don't even know your powers yet." She waved that off with a lazy sweep of her hand. "That can come later. For now, I'll finish my side of the tale."

Because this is all about you.

I bit back my words. Right now this *was* about her. I needed to know as much as I could about her. That, and she was the first person I'd come across who knew what was going on with me.

"As time passed, our worlds grew apart, the portals became fewer and harder to find. They began to shift and scatter, their locations not set, at least in our world. Most of those from the other world returned there. It was their home after all. My fellow gods and I moved on with our lives. Most of them died eventually, not having my true immortality. I used the time over the many ages to start amassing a fortune. As I saw the dawn of the modern age, I began to use that fortune, funding many projects and inventions. Some... did not do well. Alas, Tesla was just too temperamental a genius to be productive. Edison, was a much better bet. And some of my investments did very well. I'm the wealthiest person on the planet by far."

That didn't seem likely. "I think I'd have heard of you, if that were the case."

"In a way, you have." That tiger-smile returned. "I grew to like my anonymity, so I found men to play the part of princes and coal barons, the super-wealthy of their day. But they were doing it with my money. I funded them, gave them a lavish life, and in return, all they had to do was be visible. In the background, I managed their companies and properties. I'm six of the top ten wealthiest people in the world. They all work for me. Either I've bought the company they created—allowing them to keep running it as normal—or they're just actors in my employ."

Holy-fuck.

My thoughts jerked back to something she'd said earlier. "So, you stole powers from men who came from this other world—"

"And women."

Well, that was interesting. "You stole from men and women of this other world, then used them to amass wealth and power? And you want to be friends with me?"

"You make it sound like I'm some villainess. It's not like the beings from their world are truly human. They're beasts and abominations for the most part. Few of them were truly civilized. And trust me, they were well *satisfied* with our arrangement. And yes, I figured if I was going to live forever, I might as well live in luxury. What's so wrong with that?"

Nothing... and everything.

This woman was crazy. I could see that now. There

was nothing wrong with living forever in comfort, but she'd taken things well beyond comfort.

And the way she talked about the people from the other world was cold and distant. They were feeling, loving, thinking beings, not abominations. I got the feeling she'd lived with unlimited power for too long.

How did that saying go? Absolute power corrupts absolutely? I was fairly certain I was seeing that personified in front of me.

"I'm always on the lookout for more like me. You slipped under my radar for a while. Until you completely and royally fucked with my plans... twice." The vehemence in her voice was terrifying.

I leaned a little further back into the cushioned seat. Where was the door? How far away? Could I run—with Aethan's speed—to match the car so I wouldn't be tossed out onto the street? Did it matter? I could heal myself.

Her demeanor changed in an instant to flashing geniality with a harmless smile—so she did have another kind of smile.

"But I forgive you," she purred. "You didn't know of my plans. That's why I wanted to meet you, to let you know who I am, and bring you into the fold."

That sounded less like being friends and more like being her lacky.

"So that disease guy," I said. "He was one of yours?"

"Yes. He was a critical part of my plans. He created the disease and I had the cure. Once the sickness had spread around and everyone was terrified of it, I'd release the cure, and make sure everyone had a dose. I wouldn't charge much, you don't need to when you're selling it to the entire world. It was a glorious plan." She sighed. "But alas, you came along. And since he wasn't of use any more, I retired him."

One of my brows shot up. Retired? "You *killed* him?"

"Of course not. I simply let him go. I don't know who killed him. I assume he'd made enemies along the way. Perhaps one of them did him in." She flashed that genial smile again, but I didn't believe her. If she hadn't killed him, she knew who had and didn't care.

"And what do you want from me?" I asked carefully.

"Simple," she said, all disarming smiles now. "I want you to join me. I already rule this world. I figured I'd let you in on it, if you'd like. Who wouldn't want that?"

I bit back a huff. *No way in hell.*

It was the innocent and charming way she said she 'ruled the world' which let me know she was truly mad.

The question now was... what was I going to do about it?

CHAPTER 13

ANNIE

"And just out of curiosity, if I don't join you, what happens then?" I asked.

"Well, I'd let you go back to your mundane life, of course." She frowned. "Why? What did you think? I'd kill you if you didn't join me?"

Yeah, a little. "No, of course not," I lied.

She laughed, and that was just a bit terrifying.

"Annie, there's no way you can ever compete on my level. You're an inconvenience at best." That didn't seem to match with how I'd 'royally fucked with her plans.' "If you don't want to be a part of greatness, that's your choice." She leaned forward then, and all the niceties were gone from her face, the tiger returning. "Just one warning, though. Don't act against me again. That would make you my enemy. Then... I'd have to destroy you."

"And what would 'acting against you' entail?" A small part of me was tempted to do just that while the rest of me wanted to run screaming.

"To answer that, I'd have to know the complete extent

of your powers. I know you can heal. What else can you do?"

Like I was going to tell her that now. Still I needed to say something. So, I lied. But that meant quickly recalling any and all superhero movies that ex-boyfriend had dragged me to, or what was common knowledge. "I can... fly, and walk up walls... also I'm super tough and strong." Fuck, that last one was the truth. Oh well, couldn't take it back now.

"And do you plan on 'fighting crime' in any other ways in the future with these powers? Now that I know you can heal, I'll stay away from that, at least locally. You shouldn't be called out by the FBI again."

"Crime fighting? Ahhh, no, not really. I just want to live a normal life." With my four hunky roommates. Yeah... because that was *normal.*

"Then I think we'll be fine." She leaned back, the tigress gone once again and glanced out the window as the car pulled up to the curb and stopped.

"I think we're at your place," she said softly. "You can leave now." She motioned to the door.

"Ah... thanks?" I didn't know what to say exactly. I let myself out, seeing the guys piling out of the SUV behind me.

It was disconcerting that this woman knew where I lived, but she was uber-rich, so I wasn't actually surprised.

I waved to the limo as it drove away, though the windows were tinted black and I couldn't see in.

"Are you well?" Aethan asked, zipping to my side in an instant.

"I will be," I said. "Let's get upstairs."

I was a bit shaken, but felt a lot better with the guys around me. All of this was too much to take in and I needed time to digest it all.

I walked up to my apartment in a daze. I was so out of it, I just stood staring at my front door for a minute before remembering I needed keys to get in.

"You seem distracted," Rion said once we were all inside. The guys, as they did, disrobed quickly, not used to being dressed all the time.

"Yeah, I guess I am," I said, looking around at my amazing troop of guys. This caused a whole new distraction. Maybe I needed some life-altering sex to make sense of all this. And if that didn't work, at least I'd have had some life-altering sex.

The question was, with who?

That's when it hit me: Did I have to choose? If they were interested in it, could I have all of them... together... at once? My time with Del and Aethan had been my first threesome. I'd certainly never been a part of a five-some before. It felt more like some sinful orgy. Yeah, that would definitely be the distraction I needed.

"Ah..." I didn't know how to ask for it, though. "Guys... Would you all consider...?"

It was Del who saved me. "You want to be with us, *all* of us, at once?" He smiled. "You sure you'd be up for that?" He'd been serious, a bit concerned, but Aethan dispelled all of that with his next words.

"Yeah, we might just be too much for you. What's that saying of yours? 'Blow your world?'"

I giggled just a little. "It's 'blow your mind' or 'rock

your world.' But I think, right now, what I need is to have my world blown."

The guys all shared a look, then nodded. They didn't seem bothered by this at all. Something had definitely changed between them while I'd been asleep.

Keph came over and easily lifted me off my feet, cradling me in his arms. He turned toward my bedroom.

"No," I said softly. I didn't know if my bed could take all five of us and I really wanted this to be special. "We can stay out here."

Keph set me down. They all drew close then, very close. More than one of their erections brushed against me.

They helped me out of my clothes, slowly, patiently. I shivered a little once I was naked, but it wasn't from the cold. With four guys so close I wasn't cold at all. No, I was quite warm and getting hotter. The shiver was the thrill of anticipation, except I had no clue how this was going to work with the four of them.

"What would you like?" Rion asked. "Soft and slow, rough and hard?"

I wanted to savor this moment. "Let's start soft and slow. I'll let you know when I want things to change."

They moved in, hands reaching, caressing. So many hands, warm and rough, teasing over nearly every part of me.

Aethan, standing beside me, turned my face to his. Of all the men, he was closest to my height and our lips met easily. His one hand roamed over my left butt-cheek, while his other cupped my face as we tenderly kissed.

I felt him tremble, whether with anticipation or

something else, I wasn't sure, and I opened my eyes to look at him. His eyes were closed and his expression was filled with reverence, reminding me of how we bonded and how much a kiss on the lips meant to them.

I closed my eyes again, giving in to the moment, savoring the feel of Aethan's mouth on mine, and the others standing close, their bodies brushing against mine, their hands caressing and teasing me.

Long fingers slid down my belly, into my curls, and teased my opening, making heat blossom low within me but vanished just as I was getting wet.

They were quickly replaced by thicker, harder fingers: Keph. He was careful at first, then he probed deeper, searching for that magic spot. His thumb maintained a consistent gentle pressure on my clit, rubbing slow, wonderfully torturous circles, and the heat inside me grew.

Large, softer hands—Del—firmly slid up my hips and sides before wrapping around from behind and capturing my breasts. He slowly started to knead them, working my nipples into tight buds.

I released a breathy moan of pleasure and he shifted closer, pressing his hard cock against my back. The memory of both him and Aethan inside me twisted my desire tighter, and sent a shudder rushing through me.

Rion, kneeling on my other side, hummed with pleasure at my moan, his lips teasing the sensitive skin near my navel, his slender-fingered hands messaging my right thigh, inching higher and higher, closer to where Keph's fingers were starting to drive me crazy.

Gods, this was glorious. I could see how cooperation

between them could be a very *very* good thing. And it didn't seem confusing for them at all. There was no jockeying for position or awkwardness. They were working as one to tantalize and stimulate me, and it was breathtaking.

"Aethan," Keph rumbled.

I opened my eyes as Aethan's lips left mine and Keph's fingers slid away from tormenting me.

The guys were all moving, changing positions. Now Aethan was in front of me, Keph behind, and Del on my left, while Rion stayed on my right.

Keph's large fingers slid over my ass to my thighs. He grasped them, his hands easily holding me, making me look tiny and fragile, and lifted me. I leaned back against his massive, muscular chest, and he opened my legs to Aethan, who stepped close and pressed his cock against my more-than-ready opening. Then he began to vibrate.

My breath hitched and my mouth went dry with anticipation. I knew exactly what he could do with his vibrating cock, and I had to have him inside me.

But he teased me instead, brushing around my opening instead of pushing inside me.

The tremor of a climax whispered through me, and my eyelids fluttered shut as my head fell back against Keph's chest.

Oh, God, yes! And he hadn't even entered me yet.

"Annie," Rion murmured, cupping my cheek and turning my head toward him.

I opened my eyes and met his bright blue gaze. With Keph holding me, I was level with him, and he looked at me with the same awe and reverence Aethan had. A soft glow radiated from his skin and even without his wings he looked like an angel.

"You're so beautiful," he breathed and he dipped in and captured my lips in a slow, sensual kiss.

I tangled my fingers into his hair, pulling him closer, deepening his kiss and letting him see how much I loved him—how much I loved all of them.

Rion match my intensity, one hand finding my breast while Del flicked his tongue over my other nipple then sucked on it. I gasped at the sudden sting of delicious pain and Rion slipped his tongue into my mouth, any restraint he might have had, now gone.

Then Aethan finally—thank the gods, finally!—pushed inside me, scattering what little thoughts I had left.

Oh wow. Even after having experience it before, the sensation of his vibrating cock moving inside me was surprising and incredible. He worked me up even further, making me pant and moan with pleasure, before hitting that miracle spot inside me.

I came in a gasping, moaning rush as Del and Rion were both firmly grasping a breast each, hands kneading my flesh, hard and insistent.

We'd moved on from slow and soft, but I didn't care. My muscles contracted with a stunning, shuddering, trembling wave of pleasure.

"I've done my bit," Aethan said, pulling out of me. "Who's next?"

My thoughts stuttered at that. I hadn't even had a chance to give him his own release.

I didn't see what must have passed between them,

and they didn't say anything, but before I could protest Aethan stepping aside, they were changing positions again.

Now Del stepped between my legs and pushed into me with one smooth, quick thrust. Even as worked up as I was, his cock felt huge, and just that single thrust nearly made me come again.

He buried himself fully inside me and Keph nudged me forward, pressing me against Del's chest. Instinctually, I wrapped my legs around his waist and my arms around his neck, and Keph moved out from behind me and Rion took his place.

God, I hope they're going to both be inside me at the same time.

Rion boxed me in, his sculpted chest pushing me up against Del's muscled body, and teased my other opening with fingers slick with lube—Aethan must have zipped to my bedroom and gotten it while I was distracted.

I moaned louder, the sound coming out stuttering, my breath coming faster, my desire building again.

Slowly at first, Rion worked one finger then two into me, stretching me, getting me ready, and I ground down on Del, needing more, needing all of it. The anticipation was driving me crazy. I wanted them both, ached to be filled completely.

"Oh yes," I begged and Del captured my hips in an iron grip and held me steady as Rion withdrew his fingers and pushed his slickened tip inside me.

Sensation swept through me, fiery and delicious and full. It was almost more than I could handle and my body heaved, needing to move, aching to be fulfilled. But Del held tight, keeping me still as Rion inched slowly, so damned slowly, into me until he was fully buried inside me.

"Yes," I gasped. "Oh, yes yes yes." I couldn't stop repeating the word. They were perfect like this. Rion's more slender cock fit so well in behind, with Del's thicker erection in front.

Then they started moving, finding a rhythm that spiraled my need tighter and tighter, until another, small orgasm crashed through me.

But they weren't done, and even as I trembled with my orgasm, they picked up their pace. Once again I found that I hadn't reached a peak so much as a plateau on the way to incredible bliss. It felt like I just kept orgasming over and over and even still, knew some greater ecstasy awaited me.

Holy Fuck!

I gasped and moaned and tried to writhe against Del's hold, the urge to move screaming through me. But he and Rion had control of my body and unless I told them to stop—which I sure as hell wasn't—my pleasure was fully within their control.

Then large hands reached from... somewhere to cup my breasts. I didn't even know where Keph was and didn't care as he fondled my already sensitive skin. A few seconds later, his hand began to vibrate, shooting me up to my next peak with another fast shuddering orgasm that made me cry out in pleasure and left me gasping. I didn't know what Aethan was doing to help Keph, but it was working and it was wonderful.

My cry set off Rion and Del, and they came nearly at

the same time, swelling and releasing inside me, making my muscles contract in another stunning orgasm.

God, there were no words for the incredible sensation that crashed over me. It swept through every cell of my body, making fireworks explode behind my lids, and sent me spinning. I spun around and around and around among flashes of light— No I *was* the light, blazing bright, fluttering, sparking, trembling with sensation.

When I returned to myself, I was still in the throes of the most amazing, shuddering orgasm of my life, floating, moving, and carefully lowered down to straddle... Oh!

My eyes popped open—had they been closed?—and I met Keph's dark gaze.

He lay on the floor, watching me as the others helped me slide onto his massive, fully-erect, cock. My body shuddered with orgasmic aftershocks as he stretched me and rubbed against hypersensitive nerves.

I took him as deeply as I could, and he still wasn't fully sheathed, but he captured my waist with his large, strong hands and helped me keep my balance.

Another set of hands, swept around me from behind, capturing my breasts as one of the others drew close behind me, and pressed his cock against my other entrance.

My pulse stuttered and I wasn't sure how much more I could take.

Then the cock began to vibrate, and my need jerked so taut it stole my breath. All I could think about, all I craved, was to feel Aethan pushing his vibrating cock into me again.

"I love that sound," Aethan said, his breath feathering

across the back of my neck, and I realized I'd released a long, low, throaty moan as he pushed deeper inside me.

He swept a hand down my belly, and teased my clit with his fingers, but instead of staying there, he grasped the base of Keph's cock and made it vibrate as well. The two vibrating erections inside me, one so very very large, the other nowhere near as big, but in a very sensitive area, was just too much.

I cried out as I rocked slowly, back and forth, releasing wave after wave of bliss, each hitting me harder than the last, each fueled by their vibrating cocks.

Aethan slowly pulled halfway out and pushed back in, sending more waves of twitching, contracting bliss rushing through me, the sensation stealing my muscle control.

Oh God, it was incredible and too much. I was going to shake myself apart.

"Please," I begged. "Oh, please." But I didn't know what I was asking for. To stop? To finish? To keep going until I died with a silly, dazed smile on my face?

As one, Keph and Aethan, carefully moved inside me, finding their release with a few quick, shattering thrusts as if they knew I wouldn't be able to take much more. Their bodies tensed and Keph's eyes rolled back with pleasure, and a final, wave slammed over me with spinning stars and whirling darkness.

I didn't realize I'd passed out until I was coming to.

I lay on the couch, bathed in a sheen of sweat with my body aching in all the right and wonderful ways. My nerves were still hypersensitive and whispers of the most amazing climax I'd had in my life trembled through me.

The guys had all cleaned up and sat nearby, but had kindly given me space. Which was good, because I wasn't sure if just being in contact with one of them would send me spinning again.

Del brought me water and I drank thirstily. Even with that, my voice still croaked when I said, "You guys are amazing!" An aftershock swept through me, stealing my breath and making me moan in pleasure.

"We're here—" Aethan began.

"For whatever you need," Rion finished

"Always," Keph added.

And just the thought of more mind-blowing— No that had been so much more than mind-blowing. It had been world-shattering. Just the thought of more sex like that was enough to make me giggle and send another aftershock sweeping through me.

CHAPTER 14

AETHAN

Two days had passed since Annie had met Hera.

Hera. I still couldn't believe that. If there was one overarching villain in most of the tales I knew, it was her. Admittedly, she was justified in her rage most of the time since her husband, Zeus, hadn't been a faithful fellow. Though, if what she'd said in the car had been true, then Zeus may not have been her husband at all. I wasn't certain of anything anymore.

And the thought of her being out there made my skin crawl.

So, I'd been very happy to keep Annie distracted. She'd been insatiable the last few days. She'd sleep for some time, then wake, eat, and want more from us. It was clear she didn't want to think, didn't want to face what she'd learned. And the rest of us were in the same place. So, we'd kept her... busy. Not like it had been any hardship for us.

But now, after waking and having a shower, she was different, serious, pensive.

"Aethan and Keph, put on your clothes, we're going for a walk," she said, her casual command not bothering me or any of the others. Our bond with her was complete and we wanted to serve her. Which didn't surprise me. I was actually more surprised about how unsurprised I was.

"Do you need us?" Rion asked, motioning to Del.

Annie smiled, cupped Rion's cheek and kissed him then turned to Del and kissed him, too. "I will always need you. Both of you. But for this, I'll be fine with Aethan and Keph. Thank you." She looked around. "This place is a mess, though. Could you clean it up a little? I hate to ask that, but—"

"No, don't worry, we'll do it," Del replied, the words easy and quick, a demonstration of our devotion to her. I was sure as a prince he'd never cleaned a day in his life. Also, he lived in a kingdom underwater, so did that mean everything was clean all the time? I didn't know about that. Yet, he hadn't even hesitated to agree to the chore.

Once Keph and I were ready, we were out the door. Annie wore tight leggings, which really showed off every curve of her gorgeous legs and ass. Over this was a tight short-sleeved shirt, again form fitting, but unfortunately hidden by a bulky sweater which hung down to the middle of her thighs. Then she'd added her jacket as well, but even fully covered, I couldn't help seeing her naked and radiant body in my mind's eye.

Just thinking about her made me ache for her, and yet not uncontrollably. I'd had so much amazing sex recently that the thought of her didn't send me into an instant erection.

Sure, I was aroused, but I was also very satisfied at the moment. Being with Annie had helped heal my overly "lusty" nature. Of course it helped that Annie was also fairly lusty and had done her best to tire us all out these past couple days. Still, having more control and restraint with my arousal felt empowering.

"Where are we going?" Keph rumbled.

"Shopping. We need food and you all need more clothes before you destroy those nice ones I bought you. Also, I just wanted to get out and get some fresh air. I need to think." She turned to me. "Do you mind if I pick your brain?"

I was honored. "Not at all. What do you need?"

"I just need to talk. I need a sounding board and your mind is probably the quickest of the group."

I beamed at the compliment. "I'm all yours." And I was.

She was silent for a bit as we walked down the cold, slushy city street, and I could tell she was trying to figure out what she wanted to say.

Keph let us walk a few steps ahead of him. I wasn't sure if I wanted to call him up and tell him to walk on Annie's other side and join us or not. He pondered things a bit longer than the rest of us, but was very insightful at times. However the three of us walking abreast would have taken up all of the walking path—Annie had called it a sidewalk—and other people wouldn't be able to get past us.

That, and I doubted Keph would say much of anything. If he did make a comment, he'd likely make it much later once he'd had time to really think about things.

"What do you think of Hera?" Annie finally asked, her breath misting around her head.

"She's dangerous," I replied without having to think about it. "That much I know from legend. When you were speaking with her, I couldn't see her, but I felt as if... she wanted to somehow devour you."

Annie laughed. "Yeah, she had this look. I called it her tiger-face. It was this predatory look in her eyes and a smile that made me think she wanted to eat me." She was silent for a moment. When she spoke again, her voice was much softer. Annie had been much more assertive and commanding since the events at the convention center, but this tone was subdued, even timid, making my chest tighten. "I'm terrified of her."

I reached out and clasped her hand, squeezing it as we walked. Our joined hands swung between us and she squeezed back.

"We're here for you," I said to reassure her.

She looked at me, concern in her eyes. "But you heard what she said about the people from your world? How she thought of you? It was disgusting. It's like she doesn't see you as real people." She bit her lip, her golden eyes filled with worry. "I'm afraid for all of you as well, of what she might do to you."

"We can take care of ourselves. She'd have to catch me first." I grinned, hoping it was cocky and confident. Certainly, I felt fairly self-assured in that moment. I was pretty fast after all.

"Yeah... but..." She released a heavy sigh. "I lied about

my powers. She could have lied about hers, too, or not told me everything. In fact, I *know* she didn't tell me everything. Maybe she has some way to counter your speed? She's three fucking-thousand years old! She has to have ways to protect herself and deal with threats."

I didn't like where those thoughts were going. But there was something deeper going on that I wanted to address. "Annie, she said she'd leave you alone as long as you didn't go against her. Are you thinking of confronting her?"

Her gaze swept over the *cars* stopped at the intersection ahead of us, waiting for the light to turn green. "I think that's what I'm trying to figure out."

"Oh?"

"I mean, yeah, I've got everything I need right now... well except money. That's another problem I'll need to solve, but not right now. I've got some savings. So, why would I even entertain trying to go against someone like her? It's stupid. It's certainly not safe, so why am I even considering it?"

"Why *are* you considering it?" I thought I knew, but it would be more impactful if she came to the realization on her own.

"I..." Now her gaze drifted up to the tall buildings around us as if she couldn't bring herself to focus on me. "I just..."

She sucked in a heavy breath and turned her attention to me. I could see the knowing in her eyes, but also that she didn't want to put it into words. If she did, it would be real and then she knew she'd have to act on it.

"I can't... It would be stupid. I'm not... I mean I am, I

guess sort of, but really... I'm just Annie, aren't I? I know you all think I'm a goddess and all, and I did heal all those people but..." She trailed off and my chest squeezed tighter at her worry and self-doubt.

I stopped, and she stopped with me. Turning to her, I grasped her other hand to hold both of them, and locked my gaze with hers. "Just say it. You're talking around it right now, trying to avoid it. Just say it."

Her gaze went from curious to confused to solemn.

"She's evil," she said softly.

I nodded.

"And..." She grimaced. "Aethan we can't... can we?"

"Can't what? Say it Annie." I knew what she wanted to say, knew that deep inside she wanted to fight Hera because she'd been determined to heal all those people. She had a huge heart and knew Hera wouldn't stop her schemes unless someone stood up to her and stopped her.

"We can't stop her, can we? It would be silly to even try. She's so powerful. She's had three thousand years to prepare for this and I've had three weeks!"

I kept my gaze on her as Keph drew closer, a silent, steadfast guardian.

"Aethan, I know she's evil and... well, that's just it... I *know*. And the way she was speaking, I don't know if anyone else knows or cares! She's evil and powerful and she used that other guy to make thousands of people sick. She doesn't care about anyone. She's... an apex predator and she knows it. She can't be hurt by anyone except..."

I nodded. "Exactly."

In a tiny, mousy, terrified voice she said, "Except me."

"So, you're the only one who knows what she is, and you're the only one potentially with the power to stop her. So..."

Annie's eyes were a little too wide, her breath a little too fast. Even just thinking about taking on Hera terrified her.

"I have to try," she whispered. "I can't let her do what she's going to do. I don't even know what it is, but I know it's going to be evil. Well, maybe not evil but definitely self-serving and probably at someone else's expense. She was going to casually kill thousands of people, probably more! I... you're right... I'm the only one." But she didn't sound confident at all.

"You're not alone," Keph said, pressing one of his massive hands against her back.

"Exactly. You have us," I added. "She's gotten rid of her Bonded. She didn't value them. But you do, and that strength, that... love is stronger than anything she can throw at us. Together, we can defeat her."

Annie drew herself up slowly. "Gods, I can't believe I'm going to do this." Her smile was manic, the fear in her eyes shifting to a wild uncertainty.

"Do what? Go shopping?" I asked innocently.

She laughed, liked I'd hoped she would, and all her tension seemed to release. "Yeah, how could I ever go shopping!" She let go of my hands to throw her arms up in the air in mock defeat. "But I will! Gods damnit. I will go shopping!"

She laughed a bit more, smiling. It had been a joke,

but I knew what she'd really meant with those words. She'd made her choice.

It seemed she and I, and the rest of our little group, would be taking a stand against a powerful force of evil.

Now this... This was like the stories of legend.

And I was finally feeling like I might just be a hero.

CHAPTER 15

DELPHON

I SAT DOWN HEAVILY ON THE COUCH, ANNIE'S announcement weighing on me even though I knew it was the right thing to do.

"Well..." What was that word Annie used so often that even Aethan had taken to using it? Oh right. "Fuck."

Annie, Aethan and Keph had returned from their excursion, laden with clothes and food. Then they'd told us the realization Annie had come to and what it would mean. We were going to face off against a powerful ancient goddess.

"Indeed," Rion said, sitting beside me. He seemed just as surprised and stunned as I was.

"But how do we even find her?" Annie asked softly.

I pointed at Keph. "Tell her."

"Oh, right," Aethan said, realizing what I meant before the stone titan did.

Keph looked confused for a moment as everyone looked at him, then his eyes widened with understanding. "I have the sight. I may be able to divine her location."

"The sight?" Annie asked.

"It's how we knew where to find you for—" Aethan snapped his mouth shut, realizing too late he was about to mention the mess we'd made of her brother's bonding ceremony.

"The wedding?" Annie finished. "That explains a lot." She sighed. "Don't worry too much about what happened that day. It was everyone's fault, even mine. Someday I'm going to have to tell my brother the truth, but that's not today." She turned to Keph. "How does this 'sight' work?"

He shrugged his massive round shoulders. "Usually I don't want it to happen and it just comes upon me. But... I was able to draw upon it once before when needed. I'll need to concentrate for a while." He looked around. "It would help if I could have the scent of earth and stone around me."

I looked around. Annie's home had several dead plants, but that was it.

"Ah... yeah..." she said, drawing the words out in thought.

"I've got this." Aethan was gone in a flash, the door slamming shut behind him, though none of us saw him leave.

It was so sudden, we all just stared at the door for a long moment.

"I wonder what he's doing?" Rion finally asked.

"I'd guess he's going to find some earth and stone?" I replied.

"He's going to have trouble with that around here,

especially with snow covering everything. I don't know—"

The door slammed open and shut again, cutting Annie off, and Aethan appeared before us. He was huffing and sweating as he put down several buckets, then took off his jacket.

"Got it," he said.

Indeed, there were two buckets of dark loamy earth and one with small to fist sized stones.

"Where—?" Annie asked.

"When we were out for our walk, I noticed a store which had some—" He frowned. "What did they call it? Right! Gardening supplies. I went back there. I didn't have any of your little bits of plastic to pay for it, so I'm afraid I stole it, but I figured we're saving the world so..." He shrugged.

"Gardening supplies?" Annie frowned. "Hunh. Right. I don't pay any attention to it much, but yeah, we did pass a hardware store didn't we." She smiled. "Glad you're so observant."

He beamed.

I turned to Keph. "What's next?"

"Bring it here," Keph said, reaching out to Aethan before turning his attention to Annie. "This may get messy, do you mind?" He sat in the middle of her living area on the bare wooden floors.

"We're saving the world. As long as I don't have to clean it up," she said with a chuckle as if she only half meant the last part.

"I can get it done in a flash," Aethan volunteered. I

was about to offer, and, from the way Rion opened his mouth, he was too.

The cleaning we'd done around her place while she'd been out hadn't been as bad as I'd thought it might be. Handling a broom was easy, and with my powers over water, I'd summoned small streams from the bathing room to further clean the floors and some of the surfaces while Rion had worked in the kitchen, wiping and tidying the counters. Overall, it had been easy. I could get used to this simple domestic life.

"What do we need to do?" Annie asked Keph.

"Make a circle with the earth, as close as you can around me. Leave a little to put in my hands. Then do the same with the stones, placing them atop the earth."

Yeah, that was going to make a mess of Annie's nice wooden floors. We made sure any rugs were moved then did as instructed. It was done quick enough, and when we were finished, Keph sat in a stone and earth circle with his large hands cupped together before him, holding a small pile of earth and stones.

He drew in a long, heavy breath and released it, then did so again, this time lifting his hands up before his face, and closed his eyes. "This may take some time. Do as you wish, though try to be as quiet as possible please."

I looked at the others.

Yeah, we weren't going to do anything. We were all curious about this process and were going to be watching this, at least for now.

But... there wasn't much to watch. Keph sat perfectly still, his massive chest rising and falling with slow even breaths... and that was it.

After a few long, boring minutes, Aethan slipped silently over to Annie, whispering to her. She nodded and the two of them came to Rion and I.

"Once we find her, we'll need to figure out what we're going to do about it," Annie whispered to me, her breath hot on my ear, as Aethan presumably did the same to Rion. She motioned to her bedroom.

I instantly felt a stir of arousal, though I was more than satisfied at the moment. Annie's desperation to not deal with reality these past few days had been... tiring if extremely pleasant and oh so very stimulating. But I knew she didn't want to use the bedroom like that, just wanted to be away from Keph so we didn't disturb him.

I nodded and we headed into the room. It seemed smaller with the four of us crowded in there. Annie sat on the bed, pulling herself up to the top, leaning against the wall, while Rion sat at the foot, the farthest from her. Aethan sat on the top corner beside her and I took a spot in the middle.

"Soooo?" she asked, drawing the one word out. "Any thoughts?"

"What did Hera say her powers were?" Rion asked.

Yes, that would be a good place to start.

"Immortality and heightened senses," Annie said. "But I don't really know what that means. Does immortality mean she can't be killed at all or just that she doesn't grow old and die? If she can't be killed at all— Well, actually I'm not sure I want to kill her. I just want to... remove her from power."

"That can be very hard to do with tyrants," I replied. I'd read enough history of the triton people to know that much. We'd had a sordid past and there'd been a number of tyrants that had been overthrown. "Even if we remove Hera from power there may be a network of people around her that can keep her activities going without her."

"Right, so we need to stop her, then dismantle her organization." Annie frowned in frustration. "That'll take forever."

"We'll do what we can," Aethan said softly, reaching over to lay a hand on her shoulder. She smiled at that, her gold eyes twinkling just a little brighter.

"We have to assume she has more powers," Rion said stoically. "In fact, we have to assume that whatever we can do, she'll have some tactic to defend against it. She's been alive long enough to know how to protect herself."

"So, all our powers mean nothing?" Annie asked, her overwhelmed and discouraged expression returning.

"No, they mean something," Aethan said. "We'll just have to have plans to counter her plans. Luckily where she has age and experience, we have five heads to put together to figure out a way to defeat her."

"Right... Okay... Good," Annie replied, but she still seemed uncertain as if she didn't know where to start. "Gods, this is just so overwhelming!"

"I think the best plan is to try to catch her when she's alone," I said, having thought about this from the moment Annie had stepped out of Hera's *car*. "She'll have lots of lackies and guards, like that man who was outside her *car*. The weapons of this world are... violent and effective even at long range. So, we'll want to eliminate that factor since her powers will probably be more than enough for us to deal with. We won't want any other distractions while fighting her."

"That makes sense," Annie said, nodding. "Assuming that works and we can capture her. What do we do then? Where do we take her? How do we get her there? I doubt any prison on this world could hold her, and that's assuming any judge would try her."

"Our world?" Rion asked.

"No," Aethan responded quickly. "If she can bond with others from our world, that would just give her more power."

I'd had the same thought, just not gotten it out as quickly.

"Then where?" Annie asked.

"Are there any remote, secluded places on your world?" Aethan asked. "It seems there are people everywhere here."

She laughed. "No, not everywhere. Just in the cities. There are still some secluded places. So we... bury her somewhere? Drop her in the deepest part of the ocean?"

"Ocean? You have oceans?" I couldn't wait to see them, but that also meant that with my powers over water, I'd probably be able to fashion some sort of prison for her. "I could probably use my water powers to imprison her."

"So, we go in while she's alone and grab her, then take her to an ocean and trap her there?" Aethan summed up.

"That's a bit... simple, but for the basics of a plan, I think that works," Rion said.

"Without food or drinkable water, won't she just die, trapped like that, though?" Annie asked. "Maybe her immortality keeps her alive no matter what, but maybe it doesn't. We just don't know."

"Which means if we want to capture her, we'd need to commit to tending to her," Rion said. "But we will all eventually die and then what?"

Annie sighed. "You're right. I hate to say it, I don't want to kill anyone, but that may be our only option. Gods, that's horrible!"

It was and yet what did you do with a goddess who you couldn't control, couldn't contain, and couldn't make powerless?

I sighed. "We can take that burden from you, Annie. If it's our only choice, then one of us will do it."

"Thank you," Annie said, shaking her head. "It's still horrible."

Silence hung between us for a long time as we all tried to think of an alternate solution. Except even with our combined thoughts, we couldn't come up with anything. A heaviness settled over us as we came to the silent conclusion that in order to end this, we'd have to eliminate Hera for good. As Annie said, it was horrible.

"It's settled, then," Aethan said, his expression grim. "We'll discuss the details of that later without you," he said to Annie, "so you don't have to know."

She nodded, her expression just as grim as his.

"We're missing how we're going to get to and from wherever she is, though," I said. "It's not like we can just appear there by magic."

"Actually, I think we can," Aethan said slowly. "With your powers over water, can you sense where people are?"

"Yes," I replied. "In general, at least. If it's a specific person, I'd need to... have a sense for them, I think."

"Which means Annie can too."

She nodded.

"And with my speed, Annie and I can move around faster than most people can see. With Keph's strength Annie can carry each of us around. So theoretically, Annie can quickly get to wherever this woman may be, moving around people, avoiding them, and moving fast enough to otherwise not be seen while carrying the rest of you. It would have to be one at a time, but I think that could work."

That made a lot of sense. Though my pride was stung just a little at the thought of my bonded mate carrying me around like a sack of seaweed. But I'd get over it.

"Depending on where it is, I could also fly myself and someone else up there," Rion said.

"Not me!" I said quickly. Gods, flying was *not* something I wished to ever do again. That one time he'd carried me across the hall at the convention center had been enough for a lifetime. I was meant for water, not sky.

Rion grimaced. "I don't think I could carry Keph, and everyone else can move quickly."

Still, I shook my head vigorously. "Never going to happen," I ground out.

"Suit yourself." He shrugged. "Just myself then."

"So, we have ways in and out. What about actually fighting her?" Annie asked. "Alone is all well and good, but she still might be uber-powerful on her own."

"I'd like to think that a swift punch from Keph would

take her out, no matter how powerful she is," Aethan said.

Annie didn't seem convinced. "What if that doesn't do it. What if she's immune to punches? The trouble is that we just don't know. She could do anything!" Annie threw her hands up and sagged back against the wall.

"That's just it," I said slowly. "I think we have to make the assumption that she can do almost anything. And from that point try to still figure out some way to kill her. I know it seems impossible, but I don't think it is. Perhaps that means having several options on the table and going through them until one works, I don't know. But Annie is right. We have to assume that she can do pretty much anything. Because it will be the one thing we didn't account for which stops us."

From everyone's expressions, it was obvious no one liked that much, but accepted that it was the truth.

"Hey, guys," Keph called out from the next room. "I found her!"

CHAPTER 16

ANNIE

I HURRIED OUT OF MY BEDROOM WITH THE OTHERS, BUT before we could get to Keph and ask him what he'd found, my phone rang.

"One sec," I called to the others and went to my coat and pulled my phone out from a pocket to check the number. The caller was blocked. I was about to cancel the call when some instinct told me to take it. I swiped my thumb over the answer button and lifted it to my ear.

"Hello, Annie," Hera purred over the line.

I froze, my mind whirling.

"I thought I'd call and follow up on our conversation," she said, her voice was the 'tiger' tone from earlier.

I quickly tapped the mute button and called out to the guys. "Quiet, it's her!" Then unmuted and lifted the phone again.

"Uh, yeah? What do you want?" I asked, trying to sound nonchalant.

"I want you to be smart, Annie. I know you're planning to come after me. This call is a friendly reminder that that would be a very stupid idea. If you persist, my next interaction with you won't be so pleasant." A razor's edge to her voice made her already dangerous tone down right deadly. "I hope we understand each other, Annie. I'd hate to have to kill you and your precious minions. But don't mistake my one-time kindness for mercy. I have no mercy. If you go any further with your plans, you, and those savages from Eytheron, will be dead before you know it."

Fuckity-fuck-fuck!

"Ah, yeah, right, sure, I understand."

"Say the words."

"What words?"

"Say, "I know you are far more powerful than I am, Hera, and I know if I try to stop you, I will die, probably slowly, watching my precious lovers die first.' Say that."

Holy fuck this woman was pure evil.

"Ah, yeah, sure. I know you are far more powerful than I am, and—"

"Hera. More powerful than I am, *Hera*."

"Right. You are far more powerful than I am, Hera, and if I go after you, you'll kill me slowly and my guys first. Close enough?"

I could almost hear her sinister smile. "Yes. Good. I trust you now know I can tell if you're lying." A faint chuckle. "Goodbye, Annie. Have a pleasant day." Hera hung up.

I nearly dropped my phone trying to set it on the counter, my hands were shaking so hard.

"What was that?" Aethan asked. "Why did you say...?"

"She knows," I said slowly, not knowing how that was

possible, but it was. Perhaps it was one of her powers, one we hadn't considered, just... knowing everything... apparently. "Fuck. She knew and she told me to stop."

The four of them just stared at me.

"That wasn't a power I'd considered," Aethan said softly. "Long distance mind reading, or some sort of omniscience?"

"So," Keph rumbled. "What do we do now? Do you want to know where she is?"

Hell, no!

I didn't want to die. Worse, I didn't want my reckless actions to kill these four wonderful men who I loved and who loved me. I'd only just begun our relationship, complex as it was.

"Fuck," I hissed again. I didn't know what else to say.

The others slowly found seats, Rion and Del on the couch, and Aethan at my small kitchen table while Keph remained where he was. A mix of fear and frustration colored all of their expressions.

I couldn't think. Mindlessly I hit the power button on my phone to put it to sleep. The screen went dark, then almost instantly lit up again. I hit the button a second time, the same thing happened.

"What the..." I held the power button until the phone turned off completely.

A moment later it was chiming back to life.

I blinked.

My phone had a life of its own.

No...

Realization hit me. That was how Hera had known what we were doing! She'd been listening in on my phone just like I'd let the guys listen in on our conversation in the limo.

I didn't know what power that was, or whether it was just mundane hacking skills or something, but it seemed clear enough to me now that that's how she'd been spying on us. At least, it was one possible way.

Except I couldn't tell the guys, not with the phone listening.

And... I couldn't destroy the phone. That would also let her know I knew she was listening and she'd probably assume that such an action would indicate I was still going against her.

So...

Crap. Del had a phone, too.

I needed to say something, do something. "I guess that's it, guys. Sorry. We're giving up playing heroes. I guess we'll just have to go back to fucking all day." That hadn't exactly come out as I'd hoped. I left my phone on the counter and zipped—with Aethan's speed—into the kitchen where I kept my pen and pads for a shopping list. I quickly wrote down 'we're not giving up, but stay quiet' on one pad, then on another 'where's your phone?'

I zipped around to each of the guys, showing them the first note. When I got to Del, I showed him the second one as well.

His brow furrowed, then he pointed at his suit jacket, which was slung over the arm of the couch. I went over and rummaged through it, finding the phone and laying it on the couch, so it hopefully wouldn't be seen to be moving—this was assuming that whatever it was Hera was doing was also linked into the device's GPS and would know if it was going anywhere.

I nodded for the guys to follow me... quietly... into the bedroom.

Keph had trouble doing anything quietly, but managed well enough, squeezing himself through the small doorway without too much noise.

"Okay guys, time to fuck my brains out!" I called out, then closed the bedroom door.

My heart pounded, my blood rushing in my ears. If Hera had any other way of knowing what we were doing, I was about to put all of our lives at risk with my next move. I considered it for a long moment as the guys, arrayed around the room, stared at me with confused looks.

Well, fuck it.

I went to Aethan and got close, really close, my lips brushing his ear. He shivered with what could only be sexual anticipation even though it was obvious we weren't going to have sex. Man, I knew how it felt, the intensity of a breathy whisper in your ear. It made my heart race with need just thinking about it.

"I think she was listening in on our phones." I kept my voice as low as possible, barely a breath since I also knew she had enhanced hearing. "Nod, if you understand."

He nodded, his ear moving against my lips.

I waited, looking around, though I didn't know what I was looking for, nothing really. Just waiting to be struck down by lightning if she had been listening in some other way.

Nothing so far.

"We need to get everyone back to your world for a bit. I don't think she can do anything to listen in on us there."

Everything within me screamed that we should run there as fast as possible, but if she had someone watching us, that would look suspicious.

Except if I announced we were going back to the guys' world then Hera would just place someone to watch the alley for our return.

No, we had to sneak there— Or rather, zip there and hope no one noticed. Better to completely disappear. It would make Hera suspicious, but hopefully we'd be able to return unnoticed.

Except even if we did just disappear, Hera would be smart enough to have someone watching the portal which meant it didn't matter what we did, so I gave in to my desire to just run away as fast as possible.

"Can you take Del?" I whispered to Aethan.

He nodded again.

"Give me a moment to tell the others what's happening."

I went to each, whispering my plans. Aethan would take Del, Rion would fly and hopefully loose anyone watching us before meeting us in the alley. I'd take Keph, carrying him. It would be awkward, but since I possessed the same supernatural strength he did, I'd make it work.

Once everyone knew, I waited for a long moment once again.

Still no strike of lightning.

With a nod, everyone sprang into action. Aethan was gone with Del. Rion was out the window, and I sped to

Keph and picked him up, not easily, but with his strength, it was doable.

It was incredibly awkward moving with Keph. I had to set him down and manually maneuver him through doorways, but once outside, things were a lot quicker. We reconvened at the alley wall and the invisible portal to their world that only people like me and Hera could open.

It was only once we were on the other side, that I allowed myself to release a huge sigh of relief.

CHAPTER 17

HYPERION

IT WAS HARD TO RELAX. I LAY ON THE WARM SAND AS DAY dwindled and the shadows grew long. We all did, but we were also restless. We'd gone to our world to escape prying eyes and ears, but once we'd gotten here, we hadn't known what to do.

We assumed that as soon as we returned to Annie's world, we'd be targets. If this Hera was as cunning as we suspected, she had to know about the portal in the alley. She'd have someone watching it.

So then...

We had no idea. We'd all tried to think of some course of action as the day had waned, but in the end, we'd all ended up just lying there on the sand. Annie had discarded most of her clothes, while the others already been either naked or wearing very little and had stripped down the moment we'd returned.

"I could go to my kingdom and gather us an army," Del said, though he didn't sound certain. "I'd need to speak to my parents and that might not go well, but I might be able to convince them."

I could also potentially rally some of my people. I'd been away far too long, more than a week overdue to be back, but I could make excuses. I had a rank and privileges. I'd thought to give that all up for Annie, but perhaps I could still use them, except would they be able to stand against Hera?

"I don't think that would matter," Aethan said, responding to Del, echoing my unspoken thoughts. "We'd have to assume Hera has an army as well, all armed with the weapons of Annie's world. I don't think our people would do well against that. We'd only be sending them to their deaths for a cause they probably don't believe in, on a world that isn't theirs."

Exactly.

So then... What could we do?

I suddenly needed to move. I rose and began pacing. Summoning my wings, I stretched them out, arching my back and rolling my shoulders. Gods, I just wanted to fly. I always thought better riding a thermal.

"Are you going to fly?" Annie asked excitedly. She rose and came to me. The bits of cloth across her breasts and loins were alluring, hiding her treasures—even though I'd seen those treasures before—and I felt my cock start to harden

"Yes." I shook out my wings, ready to launch.

"Take me with you?" she asked drawing close, a soft hand on my chest, her light red-blonde hair catching some of the last rays of sunlight turning it into a stunning pink-gold.

Her eyes were hungry, excited, and she wrapped Keph-strengthened arms around my neck and pulled herself up to wrap her legs around my waist. Her gold eyes were level with mine, and I dipped forward to brush my lips against hers.

"Fly me," she murmured. "Please. I just need to get away." Her 'please' had been soft, urgent, heartbreaking, and accompanied by a small rock of her hips, pressing her barely covered loins against my now full erection captured between us.

Wrapping my arms around her to keep her close, I leapt and flapped my wings hard, lifting us. *Erinai* mated in flight. It was a beautiful, sensual dance, high above the earth, and while I wanted to share that with Annie, I was afraid for her. She didn't have wings and if either one of us let go or slipped—

Gods, I couldn't have her fall.

She leaned close, pressing her body against mine, our cheeks touching. "Don't worry about me. I can lift myself," she said as if she'd been reading my thoughts.

When she pulled back, she was smiling mischievously, but must have seen my scowl of confusion.

I still wasn't that high, perhaps a hundred feet up from the beach, and she released my neck and leaned back. I held onto her still, but there seemed to be little weight in my hands. When she unwrapped her legs from around me, she was... floating.

"How?" I gasped. I didn't think it was possible for her to have acquired my flight ability. That wasn't a power I'd gained by going through the portal. I'd always had it. And yet...

She laughed, lightly. "I can manipulate water, lift it. And people are mostly water."

Del's ability?

Were people mostly water?

They had lots of blood, which was a liquid. I'd never thought about it. Yet I couldn't deny she was floating in front of me.

But her smile melted away. "It's not comfortable, though. It feels like my insides want to come out, but I wanted you to know that nothing would happen if you dropped me. I can save myself."

She slid off her loin covering and drew herself back to me, wrapping her legs around my waist again and sliding her wet heat against my cock. Gods I loved that feeling, loved her heat, her soft skin, and how she completely relaxed and trusted me when we made love.

Then she reached back and removed her upper covering as well, freeing her breasts.

She wrapped her strong arms around my neck again, allowing enough space between us so I could caress her body, kneading her breasts and teasing her nipples, and building up her arousal.

With a soft, seductive moan, she leaned in and pressed her lips against mine, connecting us in the most delicious, sacred way, fueling my own desire.

We were both in too much need to play around for long, and I slipped my grip down to her hips, easing her away from me until I was poised at her opening.

Her body trembled, but from her too-fast breath and her moans of desire, I knew she shook with the same anticipation and need that blazed through me.

"Hard," she murmured against my mouth, and in one fluid motion I thrust into her, pulling her hips down to grind against mine.

"Oh, yes!" she cried out, making my balls tighten at her pleasure.

I flew higher, thrusting in and out of her quickly, building my release. I wanted to be as far away from everything as possible and be truly alone with the woman who made me feel like I was complete. She made my heart skip a beat when I saw her, and my soul ached with longing when she wasn't there.

She rocked into each thrust, crashing our bodies together, the impact almost too much with her Keph-enhanced strength. Then she tensed, legs tightening around me, with a fast and hard release.

"Oh, yes, yes, yes," she moaned, her voice thick with satisfaction.

Her muscle clenched around my cock and I gave her a second to ride the wave, sucking in my breath and fighting my own release. I knew from our three days of making love that this first one was only just a prelude to stronger, more satisfying orgasms, and I wanted to give her that.

Her release started to ebb and I slowly pulled halfway out then pushed back in again, drawing a groan of pleasure.

"More," she begged, rocking her hips into me, urging me to pick up the pace again.

Behind her, the sunset blazed with brilliant reds, oranges, and yellow, almost as beautiful as Annie, the color full and intense, like our passion.

I quickly picked up our pace again, and she threw her head back, her eyes closed, a look of pure abandon, and a little bit of desperation, on her face as if she was trying to lose herself in this moment, lose her fear and the crushing responsibility of wanting to stop a goddess.

It twisted my heart that she had to feel such fear, but I also knew that despite the fear she wasn't going to give up. My mate was strong and determined and compassionate, and if she needed to forget for just a moment, I'd give that to her.

She came again, harder than the first time, as expected, and she cried my name, pulling me over the edge with her.

We clung to each other, shuddering in the sky, high and serene, our breaths fast, our hearts pounding, our muscles locked in our release, my body barely able to keep us aloft in the most incredible way.

I managed to regain control of my flight and spun us slowly as we went through the last, glorious throes of finishing, not wanting the moment to end, but knowing it eventually would.

"The sunset is almost as beautiful as you are," I murmured against her lips, telling her the thought that had come to me while we were making love. "But nothing can truly match you."

She glanced over her shoulder to look at it. "It is beautiful. So beautiful." Then she laid her head on my shoulder and cried.

I held her close, knowing she needed this emotional release, letting her have the time she needed. There was too much at stake and it seemed no matter what we chose there was a good chance people would die.

CHAPTER 18

ANNIE

"We can't stay here forever." I'd said those words, but it didn't feel like me. I didn't feel anything like me at the moment. The 'normal' me—the one from before I'd met these amazing guys—wouldn't be standing, hands on hips, buck naked and not caring, before four hot men demanding a plan of action.

I'd come to accept being naked. It helped that when I'd discarded my underwear in a fit of passion while flying with Rion, I hadn't been able to find them afterward.

This power, this *confidence,* was a strange thing. I'd possessed it while healing the people at the convention center and the hospital, but then I'd met Hera. I'd seen her power and been terrified of it. I'd returned to my old, shrinking-violet self, and it had taken that amazing flying-sex with Rion—and some time up there to release my fears and doubts—to find this power again.

Now, I'd had a night to sleep on it and, as the sun rose, I challenged my guys.

"There has to be a way to fight Hera." It had been a statement, though part of me wanted to make it a question, adding 'right?' to the end. "Sure, she has powers we don't know about, and is probably super strong, and she has an army, but so what?" I glared at each of the guys. "Are we just going to stay here and pout about it?"

It was Aethan who said what I still feared. "We could die. *You* could die, Annie. None of us wants that."

"You're right. I don't want to die," I replied, looking Aethan straight in the eye. "What you have to ask yourself is, what would a hero do? Do they sit and do nothing in the face of danger, or do they risk death to defeat the villain?" My heart was pounding. Had I really just said that? Was I ready to die for this cause?

I could see the same question in the eyes of each of my guys.

We all thought about that for a long moment.

Was I willing to die for this?

Except could I live with myself if I didn't do it?

That answer was clear to me. No.

We were the only ones with any kind of chance of stopping Hera and there was no telling how many people she'd already murdered and how many more would die.

"I'm willing to die for this," I said. "Because I couldn't live with myself if I didn't try to do something."

Del nodded. "You're right, neither could I. I'll do it."

"As will I," Rion said, his expression somber.

"And I," Aethan added.

"And that means I have to go to keep you all from dying," Keph said so seriously it took me a moment to realize it was a joke.

I laughed, as did the others, but it didn't last. Too much was at stake.

"Good, now that that's settled, what's the plan? Same as before? Something tells me Hera's going to be expecting us now. That and she may not be alone that often, if at all."

"I think the plan is the same," Aethan said considering, eyes downcast, staring at the sand. "She may not be alone, but she can't be surrounded by an army at all times, not too closely anyway. There has to be moments when she's at least minimally guarded."

Rion huffed out a sigh. "Still."

"Still?" I asked.

"We just don't know enough. How did she know what we were planning? What are her powers? If she just *knows* things, then how will we ever hope to surprise her?"

Del sat up a little straighter suddenly. "There might be a way to know."

We all looked at him. He himself seemed a bit surprised. "I don't know why I didn't think of it before." His expression of enlightenment shifted to one of chagrin. "Perhaps because I'd accepted I was never going home again."

"Just because you're bonded to me, doesn't mean you can't go home. I'd never do that to any of you," I said, wondering where this strange thought from Del had come from.

Everyone looked at me now.

What had I said?

"We never told her, did we?" Rion said slowly.

"I'd meant to," Del replied sheepishly.

"Tell me what?"

Del stood and gave a very formal bow. "Annie, I am Delphon of Galniosia, Prince of the Realm and heir to the Pearl Throne."

I gaped.

Fuck me! And he had... several times. And it had been wonderful. I shuddered blissfully with the memories. I was bonded to a prince!

Suddenly, every girlish fantasy I'd ever had of being swept off my feet by 'prince charming' returned to me and I was that giddy school-girl again. "A... prince? My very own prince?"

"Well, yes and no."

"No?" My school-girl hopes sputtered out.

"By bonding with you, I've dedicated myself to you and I can't accept my responsibilities back home. I have to abdicate. That's why I can't return. If I do, I'll have to have a very awkward conversation with my parents. My little brother will be happy though, he gets to be the next king." He blew out a long breath. "So, I'm sorry, but I have to give up being a prince."

Oh... I was okay with that. A prince who'd give up his position of power for a girl like me? That was among several of those girlish fantasies.

"I can accept that," I said. "Going back, though. You said there might be a way to know Hera's powers? I'm guessing it involves going home? What is it?"

He nodded. "Right. Ah... well, my old tutor was also the curator of the library of Galniosia. That old woman knew everything there was to know about... well, everything, including the ancients. And if she didn't know it, she knew a book where she could find out about it. There has to be something in that library. It's the largest in all of Nikandra."

"He's right," Aethan said. "Anything my people have pales in comparison. We don't even have books, just an oral tradition handed down by elders."

There was something about the words 'oral tradition' that made me think of Aethan's face between my legs, and I fought to hide my expression at the thought. Gods, but I had a dirty mind!

"Then let's go!" I said, struggling to stay on topic. "Del, lead us to your library and this tutor of yours."

Again, everyone was looking at me.

"What?"

"Can you breathe water?" Keph asked.

"What? No. Why?"

"Neither can the rest of us, except Del," Aethan said.

"And?"

"And, my kingdom and this library are underwater, Annie. I'm a triton remember. I live in the seas."

Oh.

I searched my memory. Had he told me that? If so, I'd forgotten with everything else that had happened. I knew he was a merfolk, but I'd never made the connection that his home might be underwater. I guess I'd assumed it was on an island somewhere since he could easily turn his fishtail into legs.

"So, how do we get there?" I asked. "Is there a way?"

Everyone turned their attention from me to Del.

"There is, but it's not particularly pleasant."

Aethan's eyes suddenly went wide. "You don't mean huphelopoids?"

"I do."

"Fuck." Aethan drew out the word. Whatever this 'Hufflepuff' was, apparently Aethan agreed that it was unpleasant. The look on his face was one of disgust mixed with morbid curiosity.

"What's a huphelopoid?" Keph asked as Rion frowned, his expression making it clear that he didn't know what it was, either.

Del gave a grimace. "Follow me." He began walking toward the town of Masia. "We'll need to catch a boat. There's only one island in the archipelago where you can find them. I'll... explain along the way."

Somehow, I didn't think I was going to like this explanation.

CHAPTER 19

"THAT'S DISGUSTING!"

Del had just fully explained the 'Hufflepuffs' and yes, they were really called huphelopoids, but my mind really wanted to call them Hufflepuffs. Too much Harry Potter as a kid, I guess. And now that I knew what they were and what they did, the "puff" seemed more than adequate to describe them.

"On your face?" Rion asked, looking as disgusted as I felt.

We all stood on the docks, waiting for the small ship we'd hired as it prepared for departure. I was still naked and unashamed about it. It helped that all the guys were too, as was everyone else in the village, and no one made a big deal about it. It was strange, but that was the way of this place. When you lived in a tropical climate, you didn't really need clothes, especially if the idea of physical modesty just didn't exist in the culture. And to be honest, it was kind of liberating.

"Yep," Aethan said, also looking a bit sick at the prospect.

"And they breathe air and water and carbon dioxide?" I asked. It seemed the understanding of the elements here wasn't as clear as on my world. My use—and then explanation—of the words 'carbon dioxide' had stunned all the guys.

"I don't know all the details," Del said. "I've never had to use one. But whatever we breathe in and out, they seem to be fine with. From what I've heard, they live happily on shorelines, half in and half out of the water. It was some adventurous nymph who tried them first and found out if you allowed them to latch to your face, covering your mouth and nose, both you and the huphelopoid would survive just fine. It's a symbolic relationship."

"I think you mean symbiotic," Aethan corrected him with a chuckle.

Del rolled his eyes at him. "Whatever, yes."

"And they have tentacles, like squid?" I asked.

"Yes. That's how they clasp onto your head. You may have little suction marks on your face for a while afterward, though. I've heard that happens if you wear them for a long time."

"Great." I was going to have to stick a squid to my face and breathe into it to go underwater. That was a wonderful fashion statement. Especially going to see the parents of one of my guys. *Royal* parents at that.

Yeah. That would be a meeting of the in-laws I'd not soon forget. *Uh, yeah, hi your highnesses, pardon the squid on my face.*

Just the thought was making me queasy, though that could have also been the soft rise and fall of the floating dock we were standing on, too. I wasn't much looking forward to this boat ride. I'd been out on Lake Michigan all of once on a boat that belonged to my ex's parents. That had not gone well. I'd had my head over the side, losing my lunch, for most of it. Another wonderful interaction with potential in-laws. At least I was consistent.

The captain waved at us, indicating the boat was ready and we boarded. The crew, all minotaurs, big and brawny, were all larger than my guys except for Keph—no one was larger than Keph... well, no one I'd met yet—and they rowed us out a bit, then unfurled the sails and we were off, skipping across the water.

Surprisingly, my stomach was fine.

But then, I did have healing powers and powers over water now. Perhaps that was what was saving me.

It turned out, sailing was quite lovely when you weren't puking over the side of the boat. Aethan, however, turned a bit green, and I used my powers to calm his uneasy stomach. We sat on the benches off to one side at the rear of the boat, and he curled close to me, laying his head in my lap as I stroked his temple. It was intimate and endearing without being sexy, and it only really occurred to me then that I'd bonded with these four guys without really knowing them. Most of the time we'd spent together had been either dealing with a crisis or... bumping like bunnies.

"I know this may sound weird after all we've been through," I said to them. "But I know very little about all of you. I didn't know Del was a prince. That feels like something I should have known. Tell me about yourselves."

"To be fair," Del said, "I only just told the guys I was a prince a few days ago."

"But we already knew," Aethan said from my lap. "It was easy to tell from how he always glorified tales of 'his prince' when he spoke to us. There was a gleam in his eye. An 'I'm talking about me' sort of gleam."

Del sighed. "Well, there's one thing about me, apparently I can't keep a secret or tell a lie convincingly."

"Not to people who know you anyway," Rion said.

They were all quiet for a moment after that.

Finally, Rion sighed. "Where to start..."

"Tell me about your families," I said softly. But then... they didn't know about mine. This whole 'get to know you' thing would have to go both ways.

"Mine are good folk in general," I said, willing to start us off. "They just never really understood me or what I wanted. My dad's a doctor." Rion frowned, reminding me that they didn't use the same words I did for certain things. "That's a healer, but without powers. I think you have those here, right?"

The guys nodded their understanding.

"My mother was the same." I had no clue how to make the distinction between a doctor and a nurse to them so... yeah. "And in my world, you make a lot of money doing that. But I didn't want to make money, well I do, but I didn't need to be rich like they were. I wanted to live a simple life, somewhere warm."

"It's warm here," Keph said, turning his face to the sun, his eyes closed, soaking it in.

"It is. It's wonderful here. I'm tempted to stay here... when this whole Hera thing is over, that is," I replied.

"Not your world? I thought we'd live there," Rion said.

"I'd rather live here, if you're all good with that."

The guys exchanged odd looks and I had no idea what it meant.

"That would require a lot of explaining to our various families and clans," Rion said.

"I'd have to explain why I'm living with four guys to my friends and family in my world." I shrugged. "We'll all have to explain it eventually to everyone."

From their reluctant nods, it was clear that was a truth none of us wanted to face anytime soon.

"Anyway, my family. My brother is—" Did they have accountant's here? "He works with numbers and my sister is a florist. She works with flowers. They're all very successful at what they do. And I... well, I had a job where I was doing well, before you all came along. Now that's gone." I held up my hand to stop them, their apology for me losing my job clear in their expressions. "I'm fine with it. It just means I'll have to start my own business all the sooner. It's what I'd planned on doing."

"If you do stay here, a healer with powers like yours would be welcome in any society. People would be happy to pay, those that could. You'd do very well," Keph said, his eyes still closed, his face to the sun.

Hunh. That was an interesting option I hadn't thought of.

"That's my family. I love them and they love me, but we've never really understood each other. As for friends... I have a few." The sad truth, though, was that none of them were close. I was an introvert. I liked snuggling on the couch in my apartment and watching a good rom-com.

I'd had a few acquaintances through work, but if I was honest, I probably wouldn't keep up with them, now that I'd left.

There were a few other friends from childhood, but they lived across town or in different states now and that group had moved apart, growing into their new lives as adults. We met up, one-on-one, every now and then, but we very rarely met as a full group anymore. Some of us might get together around the holidays, but it had been years since everyone had been there.

"I'm not really close to any of my friends." A wave of melancholy swept through me as I realized that my distance from my family and how they'd treated me and my dreams meant I'd never really felt comfortable sharing myself with others. I'd kept things light and fun with my friends, not letting them see the real me. Now, I was alone and no one really knew me.

Well, no, I wasn't alone. I was surrounded by four hunky guys, and they were far more than just man-meat. I could see in their faces a reflection of my own sadness as I spoke. I was getting the feeling they were all like me, distant from the family and friends who were supposed to know them.

Gods, how had I gotten so lucky to find others who were so much like me.

I smiled. "Now I have you four though, and that's all I really need."

CHAPTER 20

HYPERION

"Now I have you four though, and that's all I really need."

Annie's words sank into my soul, a balm on all the pain I'd bound deep within me. I could see the pain in her expression as she'd spoken of her family and friends and it had echoed that same ache in my soul. We were kindred spirits, fated, meant to be. How else could her words speak to me so deeply?

"I feel the same," I said softly. I looked around at my three best friends and my bonded love. "I don't think I've known anyone as well as I've known you three. I don't know how you feel, but you're like brothers to me."

They all nodded. Keph did so without opening his eyes or adjusting the relaxed, upward position of his head.

"Brothers," Aethan said. I felt a touch of envy for the man, his head resting on Annie's thigh, though I understood his sickness and dislike of water. I was used to the high buffeting currents of air, much like the waves over which we now crashed, but he was from the plains and wouldn't have had a lot of experience with either wind or water.

"The others know some of this, but not all. Perhaps it's time I spoke about my life," I said.

Annie smiled a smile that brought so much warmth and peace to the layers of turmoil within me. It always did.

"I was raised with a certain amount of privilege. The *erinai* don't have much in the way of poverty, all people are integrated and work is found for everyone that best suits their abilities." I frowned. "Well, there are some who are looked down upon: the aged and infirm, who we literally look down upon because they can't fly. They're well-tended, but we all feel that their lives must be torture, to be born to the skies but not able to reach them anymore."

Del shuddered. "I can't imagine how horrible it would be to not be able to swim in the sea."

"Another reason I think it would be better if we lived here," Annie said.

"Anyway, my father is the Sky General, the leader of the *erinai* military. I was trained well, though not by him. He was always away on missions or in meetings with the Sky King. Even when he was at home, he was aloof, and hard to know. Hard in general."

I fought a shudder thinking about the cold, distant way he looked at me... at everyone. I wasn't even important enough to be looked at differently than anyone else.

"He's a stern man, even with my mother and my sister: rigid, no room for question, and old fashioned in his thinking. A woman's place is in the home, married, tending children. Yet my sister, Ehlana, wished to be in the military." Gods, that had been a terrible fight. And worse when he'd discovered the truth. "Father forbade it. So, I trained her. When Father found out he was furious. He sent her away to a school for girls and arranged a marriage for her as soon as she was old enough."

"That's horrible," Annie gasped.

And it got worse. "She died a husk of her former joyous self a few years later." My throat tightened. I'd never told anyone that, not even the guys, mostly because just thinking about it always infuriated me and tore at my insides. I clenched my jaw, trying to keep my emotions in check, but a tear escaped my control and rolled down my cheek. A part of me wanted to just weep openly, but that was another thing that had been—literally—beaten out of me. Men didn't cry.

"Oh, Rion," Annie murmured, reaching out to me.

I accepted her hand, savoring the feel of her soft skin and firm grip, knowing in just that simple gesture that she'd always support me. We might not agree on everything, but she'd never be cruel like my father and she'd always listen to my opinion.

Del placed a hand on my shoulder. "I don't know the pain you must carry from this, but—" He glanced at the others who all, even Keph, looked at me. "I know this, we've all been cast out from the places that raised us. Our pain may be different, but this is the same."

I knew enough of the tales of the others to know this was true.

Annie gave a soft, sad laugh. "So, we're *all* outcast then?"

"We are," Keph rumbled, his voice solemn.

"My troop of outcasts," she replied, giving each of us a tender, loving smile.

"Bound to you, bound as brothers, bound by our banishment, self-imposed as it may be," Del said. The poetry of his words caught like a bur in my mind and soul. I nodded. Looking at him, I put a hand on his shoulder as well.

"Bound as brothers," I repeated.

"Brothers," Keph and Aethan said as one.

After a long moment, Annie asked, "Is there more to your tale Rion?"

I sighed. "That's the bulk of it. My mother is always compliant with my father's wishes. She's... worn, aged beyond her years from dealing with him. I—" My emotions swelled again. This was the truth that frustrated and hurt the most. "I might wish to go back and free her from his grasp, but I honestly don't know if she'd go. She's been under his influence for so long, I think she's accepted her fate. It pains me to say it, but if I tried to take her away, she'd probably run right back to him. I don't know if there's anything I can say to reach her."

"Some women, even though they know they're in a bad place, fear leaving. They may even live with it for so long that it seems more painful to leave than to stay. All we can do is try to help, understand that it's a difficult situation, and be patient with them." She squeezed my fingers and offered me a soft smile.

"As for friends, I had few, and most were in the military," I said. "They revered my father and I'm afraid they wanted to get close to me so they could get close to him.

Either that or they knew I might someday replace him and were seeking positions of power when that day came. Those sorts sicken me. The one true friend I had growing up, Eordal, was injured during a battle with some wild griffins. He lost the ability to fly and that broke his spirit. He died about five years ago now."

"More tragedy," Annie said. "I hope that's not all you've ever known."

I smiled, even if it was a wan, sad thing. "It's not." I glanced at Del. "Eight years ago, I met my brothers and that has been a joy in my life ever since."

Keph grunted his agreement and Aethan and Del smiled and nodded.

I let out a long, heavy breath. "That's my tale. Who's next?"

"Perhaps, since we're headed there," Del said. "I should tell you more of Galniosia."

CHAPTER 21

DELPHON

I'D MADE THE DECISION TO STAY WITH ANNIE AND GIVE UP my life as a prince, and the thought of returning to the beautiful city of Galniosia filled me with conflict. I wished to see it, even if only one last time, but I knew there would be some hard conversations to come. I kept telling myself 'better now than later,' but that wasn't helping much.

"In my opinion, there isn't a more beautiful city in the world," I said wistfully. "Especially when the midday light filters down and washes over the towers and swaying stands of giant kelp." I sighed, closing my eyes to bring the sight to mind.

"How far down is it?" Annie asked.

"The lagoon here in the archipelago isn't that deep. Galniosia is at the center of it. There's a trench that runs through the west side of the city which falls to about two hundred feet, but the city itself isn't much more than a hundred feet down.

Opening my eyes to look around, I peered down into

the waters. "On a clear day you can see it. We're not far away now. The path to the island we're going to won't take us directly over it though."

The waters were a bit choppy today as well, a stiff wind helping to make the sailing journey that much faster.

I turned back to the others. "My people aren't perfect. There are some tritons who live with little. They hunt for their food and live off the kelp and algae when hunting isn't so good. There's food aplenty, that's not the problem. There are simply few opportunities for those not born to power or wealth. Trade routes with the surface have been established and contracts are rarely broken. There aren't many raw resources to mine or work with, so crafters are generally scarce. The few there are, are generational now, passing down their craft from father to son or mother to daughter. New blood is rarely introduced. It's... static. Things rarely change beneath the waves."

That was one of the things that frustrated me the most about my people, and I knew any kind of change would be slow, take an enormous effort, and a powerful leader. And while I wasn't opposed to the effort and could be patient with things that were important to me, I knew enough about myself that I wasn't a charismatic enough leader to evoke meaningful change.

"We're perhaps a bit more progressive than the *erinai*," I said, glancing at Rion. "Though that's only because we had a queen as a ruler before our current king and she did much to progress the rights and liberties of women."

The previous queen—my grandmother—had been a

true force to be reckoned with and whenever I thought about a true leader, I thought of her, someone with whom I'd never be able to compare.

"Yet, there was little that could be done for those who didn't have some form of power already," I continued. "There just aren't positions to give them. It's like a picture, beautiful, but unchanging." And nothing I could do about it.

I pushed aside my melancholy. It was what it was. "But, all that aside, we do care for our people. There's no rent or need to purchase land. People live for free. There are no taxes on those who aren't making a certain amount, so they can at least remain where they are. And where we're going, you'll see the Palace of Pearls and the Hall of Light." Which brought me to the not-so-fun part. "And you'll meet my family."

Annie let go of Rion's hand and reached out for me in silent support.

I took it, savoring the feel of her soft, delicate fingers interlaced with mine. A part of me was still amazed that she'd picked me, even though a stronger part of me deep within my soul, knew we belonged together, we all did, and us bonding was destiny. Maybe that was why I'd never felt like I belonged on the throne.

"Despite being king, my father is nothing like yours, Rion. He's a jovial, easy-going fellow. It's been over a hundred years since there was any strife or war among my people. He's a fair ruler, but in truth it's my mother that's the true power on the throne. She was handpicked by the previous queen to marry her son. She was tutored and trained to be a woman of power." I grimaced. "If I have trouble with anyone in my family, it's her. She expects a lot from all her children. She says that 'because we're royals, we have a duty to be and do more than those we serve.' I've never quite lived up to that for her."

"I don't know if that's better than having no expectations of yourself or not," Aethan said, reminding me that his exile was self-imposed. His people didn't understand him, nor he them.

"My mild-mannered brother is intelligent and artistic. He took to governance the same way he took to sculpting. He's taken to everything put before him and remains quiet and humble. That's the son my mother wanted. She smiles when she looks at him."

"I'm pretty sure that's the son every mother wants," Rion said.

"Or daughter," Annie added, and from what she'd said, I knew she understood how much it hurt not living up to her family's expectations.

My jaw tightened. It had been a long time since my mother had smiled when she looked at me.

"My sister is also another near-perfect child," I said. "Despite being ten years younger than I, she's already exceeded me in every way that counts to my mother. She's poised and strong, knowledgeable and quick of mind. She loves playing games of strategy and regularly beats our own generals. She'll probably lead our army one day, small as it is. If she has a fault, it's that she's strong willed and challenges my mother on occasion... or did, when she was a youth, not so much anymore."

And I wasn't sure if that was because she'd given up challenging our mother or realized it was smarter to just step around the confrontation and do what she wanted anyway.

I blew out a long, heavy breath. "I just..." I shrugged. "I didn't want any of that! I wanted to be free! It's not like I'm not-responsible or willing to put in the work, I just hadn't found anything I wanted to put work into until I met you guys. And you, Annie." The entire reason I was returning home was so we could research a goddess we were about to fight. "I never saw myself as a hero or warrior, but I'll fight for all of you. I'll do what needs to be done to rid your world of this Hera."

And there it was. I'd fled from responsibility and rulership, only to find myself dedicated to freeing a whole other world. I wondered if that would please my mother or disappoint her more?

"I never doubted your nobility," Annie said, her gaze soft yet still determined.

"I did. Often," Aethan said from her lap, but he smiled kindly, his words clearly a joke, and the others laughed with us.

"Will they help us?" Annie asked.

That was the question. "I have no idea. They'll certainly be upset with me, expect that much. I've been gone far longer than I should have been. They don't get many outsiders in Galniosia so I'd expect the rest of you would be more... curiosities than points of contention. They're good people, so I suspect they'll help *you*." I made sure I put emphasis on the *you*.

"And what will happen to you?" Annie asked concerned.

"I'll renounce my title." I shrugged. It was a whole lot easier to say than it would be to do. Well, that wasn't true. All I had to do was say those words again formally, but there would probably be a lot more of a discussion with my parents—specifically my mother—around it.

"And will that cause any problems?" Annie asked, although I suspected she'd already figured out the answer.

"For me, no, not in the long run. For my mother, it will be a huge problem. Well, maybe not a problem so much as it will confirm her problem child is an irredeemable lost cause." I gave a fake smile. A part of me thought of myself that way still, a part which had been ground into me by my mother.

"She can't really see you that way. You're her son," Annie said.

"I'm her biggest failure. It's a sore spot for her, I think."

Annie frowned. I guess she didn't much like that, but didn't know what to say. I couldn't blame her. I'd felt that way most of my life.

I shrugged again. It was all I could really do. "Don't worry about it. It's my burden to bear, and it will all be over and done with soon. Then we can get back to defeating an immortal goddess."

That thought brought everyone back on track, drawing us into a grim silence. No one said much after that.

When we arrived at the island, Keph hopped out of the boat first and instantly sunk a good foot into the soft sands. He looked down at the shallow water lapping around his knees then back up to us. "Is now a bad time to mention I can't swim?"

CHAPTER 22

ANNIE

I JUMPED OVER THE SIDE OF THE BOAT EVEN BEFORE IT HAD come to a full stop. The waters lapped around the top of my hips, warm and refreshing, and for a second I was awed at how amazing this island was. It was a tropical paradise with turquoise water and pale sand, matching the picture I had in my head of where I wanted to live.

I dove beneath the shallow water and swam around for a moment, noticing the many small to medium sized fish as well as several odd-looking octopus like things. Perhaps these were Hufflepuffs?

I surfaced a short distance down the beach, in time to hear Keph say, "Is now a bad time to mention I can't swim?"

I swam over to him as he trudged heavily out of the water.

"It's easy," I said, "I can teach you."

Rion laughed and shook his head as if he'd just realized the obvious and couldn't believe he'd missed it. "I don't think Keph is saying he doesn't know how to swim, though I suspect that's also the case. Look at him. He physically *can't* swim. He's not buoyant enough. I don't know why none of us thought of it until now."

Oh... yeah, right. He was heavy as a brick wall and build like one too. He'd sink like a stone.

"Well, is that a problem?" I asked. "Can't he just walk there?"

"He could," Del said, "but there's a lot of uneven ground underwater and it would take him some time to get there."

"We could have the boat go back and drop him in closer to the city," Aethan suggested.

"That *could* work," Del said then frowned. "Ah, no. Not a good idea. He'd have to walk out. None of us would be able to carry him while swimming, and that would also take a long time. No, sorry Keph, but you're right, I don't think you can come."

The large, onyx skinned man, shrugged and rubbed his hand over his bald head. "Oh well. I'll visit your city some other time. Although the thought of being under water, always... worried me just a bit anyway. If that thing came off my face, I'd just... well I'd have nothing I could do. So, it's probably for the best. I'll meet you all back at the rocks on the beach near Masia," he said, signaling the boat to come back and get him.

"We'll miss you," I said, swimming to his side and hugging him as best I could, since my arms couldn't reach around his massive body.

He knelt and we shared a kiss, as soft and tender as was possible with Keph. I lingered with him for a long moment, letting him know just how much I'd miss him, and was breathless when we finally drew apart.

"Stay safe," I murmured.

"And you," he replied, sliding a large hand down my naked back and cradling my butt, making me more than just a little hot.

He quickly kissed me again, then turned to the boat, as if he wouldn't be able to stop himself from going farther with me if he didn't leave right away.

I blew out a long, warm breath, trying to bring myself down from this new, aching heat as I watched Keph climb aboard. That was a show in itself, his heavy form nearly capsized the small craft. The minotaurs were experts at their trade, however, and managed to help him aboard while keeping the boat afloat.

He waved as the boat sailed away, and I felt like a part of me was being slowly pulled away with him. I sagged to my knees in the shallow water for a long moment, simply trying to breathe against the tightness in my chest. Since we'd bonded, I'd never been that far from any of my guys. I hadn't expected such a physical reaction and yet it made sense. They shared their powers with me, which meant our connection was deeper than just being in love. It was a soul to soul connection, bound by magic, and it squeezed tight with the fear that I didn't know how long we'd be in Del's kingdom or when I'd see Keph again.

Gods, Hera must be one cold-hearted bitch to have killed those she'd bonded with. Just being separated from Keph hurt. I couldn't imagine the agony of him dying or our bond being severed.

"Annie, are you all right?" Aethan asked.

I shoved up to my feet, rubbing my chest as if that would somehow ease the ache of Keph's absence. "Yeah."

I had to push onward even though it felt like I was missing a limb or something integral to my being. Keph couldn't come and we had to learn more about Hera. It was our only way to survive facing her—because I knew in my soul I wouldn't be able to let her continue killing people in my world or the guys' world.

Del offered me a soft smile and transformed into his merfolk form, flicking his massive tail out of the water and splashing Aethan, making the *satyr's* red mohawk flop in his eyes before diving under the water.

Those odd octopus-like things I'd seen were indeed the huphelopoids, and Del, lithe and quick in the water, caught three of the slippery things and handed one to each of us.

I stared at the squirming mass of goo and tentacles in my cupped hands, unable to make myself bring it to my face.

Rion was the bravest of the three of us, and just did it. The huphelopoid sent tentacles around behind his head and seem to snuggle close around his mouth and nose. He made a face, though I could only see his eyes, which still conveyed discomfort and disgust and didn't inspire much confidence.

Aethan glanced at me then down at the suction-cups and the weird sponge-like part which was supposed to go over his mouth and nose.

I glanced at mine. This was the only way. And while a small part of me said Del could go get this information himself or with Rion, a much larger part of me didn't want to be separated from another of my guys and didn't want Del to have to face his family alone.

"Ah, fuck it," I hissed and pressed the thing against my face before I could chicken out.

It smelled foul, and my eyes watered as my nose sank into its spongy body. It wrapped its tentacles around my head just like Rion's had done and pulled close and for a moment, panic seized me with the sudden fear that I wouldn't be able to breathe. But then I gasped in a full breath, a breath which reeked of salt and fish, and made me gag. I fought through the sensation, uncertain it I'd even be able to throw up with the thing on my face, and managed to draw in another, steadier breath, then another.

I turned to Aethan and—

Hunh. I didn't know if we could talk in these things. I could move my mouth and breathe in and out like normal, but I didn't know if that meant I could talk or if the others would be able to hear me.

"Can you hear me?" Rion asked, as if he'd known what I'd been trying to figure out. His voice was muffled, but I could hear him well enough.

"Yes," I said. The huphelopoid vibrated a little on my face as I spoke, making me wonder if they somehow amplified the sound, but I pushed that thought back. It wasn't really important. I had superpowers so it made perfect sense that I'd be able to talk and breathe under-water with an octopus thing on my face.

"I feel like I'm going to regret this," Aethan groaned as he drew the huphelopoid to his face. He sucked in a deep breath—that I knew smelled of fish—half coughed half gaged and jerked the creature away before its tentacles could latch onto him. "Oh gods, yes."

"You get used to it," Rion said, his expression perfectly normal as if the huphelopoid didn't bother him at all.

"*You* got used to it. I'm not sure I will," Aethan shot back.

Del rolled his eyes at him. "Just do it. We're wasting time."

Aethan tried again, this time lasting long enough for the thing to attach itself. He seemed to cough into it a few times, sounding like he was choking, his eyes wide, but eventually the coughing subsided and his eyes narrowed.

"This is disgusting," he groaned. "Come on, let's get this over with."

"What if one of these things just decides to detach itself and swim away while we're down there?" Rion asked, wading deeper into the water until it was chest high.

I had to admit, I hadn't thought of that, and now that I had, I didn't much like the thought.

"Remember, the city isn't that deep. At most we'll be perhaps a hundred feet down. That takes less than a minute to swim." Del was trying to be reassuring.

"For you maybe. You've got a fish tail. I don't," Aethan said, as Rion dipped below the water for a few seconds then popped back up.

"True. But don't worry," Del said. "I can help you to the surface and assist you in breathing while we go."

My pulse stuttered at that, and the image of our lips locked as he helped me breathe flashed through my mind's eye. Then the image jumped to Rion and Aethan lip-locked with Del, which turned me on and made me giggle.

I sank below the water like Rion had to try breathing with the creature on my face and to hide my laughter, and took a few unsteady breaths.

While the guys hadn't had a problem having sex with me at the same time, I had a feeling, they wouldn't be as excited as I was to be mouth to mouth with Del in order to breathe.

"—never heard of one of these things coming off without a bit of work, though," Del reassured us as I resurfaced. "You'll all be well enough."

And with that, a few false starts to get used to breathing with the things on, and just a bit of apprehension, we dove down, heading out into the lagoon.

It was amazing to watch Del swim in his triton form, so quick and powerful. He was literally swimming circles around us so as not to get too far ahead.

It was then I knew we would never be able to stay in my world, at least not in Chicago. Del needed to be where he could swim, and Rion where he could fly and Aethan where he could run. They wouldn't have that in my world.

No, if they were going to be their best selves, I'd have to live here with them.

And while I was a bit sad about that, I wasn't entirely heartbroken. Their world was a tropical paradise after all... if Hera didn't turn her attention to it, which, now that she was aware of me, seemed unlikely.

CHAPTER 23

AETHAN

THERE WAS A SAYING: LIKE A FISH OUT OF WATER. THERE
should have been a similar one: like a horse in the ocean.
I felt just as out of place in the water as I was sure a fish
did on dry land.

We'd been swimming for what felt like forever before
Del started to get agitated and excited. Then we reached
a tall stand of sea-weed that rose dozens of feet high like
an underwater forest.

"Just through here," Del said.

We swam through it and stopped just on the other
side to stare in stunned silence at Galniosia.

Del had been right. The city was beautiful... I just
wished it was on land.

Sunlight filtered from above in rippling waves, shimmering over the city. It gleamed off pearl-white towers,
thin and tall, as well as the myriad of lower buildings.
And not just the palace, but all of the buildings. They all
sparkled in a spectacular fashion, and as we drew closer, I
could see there were shells pressed into the sides and

tops of the structures, catching the sunlight and shimmering in various colors.

"Oh, wow," Annie gasped, her voice muffled by the huphelopoid on her face.

"Welcome to Galniosia," Del proclaimed brightly, before his expression fell into grim determination. "Time for me to face my family."

We swam to the palace, a towering complex structure, with large windows that were more like doors with people coming and going from them... or were they really doors and I just thought they were windows because there were so many of them and they weren't on the ground.

Although if I really thought about it, the function and design of a building could be quite different under water, where people could swim to any floor with ease.

The central part of the palace had a large landing with a garden of rocks and various colored corals with small, bright fish darting about.

We were met by guards, who stood before an opening larger than any of the openings I'd seen, and were quickly admitted inside.

There was a flurry of activity as soon as Del's arrival was announced with other guards called forward then sent off, quickly swimming to tell whoever was supposed to know that he'd returned and servants gathering in the corridor, waiting to be commanded.

A heavy-set man with a wide, blue-green tail and the air of someone who thought he was more important than he really was, darted down the hall to greet us like one of the fish I'd seen in the coral outside despite his girth.

"Welcome home, your highness," he said, his tone verging on condescension as his gaze slid over us then jerked back to Del. "Should I have rooms prepared for your guests?"

"No, I need to speak with Archivist Umandra as soon as she's available. I'm guessing my parents will also want to see me. Might as well get that out of the way as well." He looked at us and grimaced. "We won't be staying long."

Yeah, I didn't want to spend any more time with this squid attached to my face than was absolutely necessary. Sleeping with it on was out of the question. I was sure I'd never relax with it stuck to my face long enough to even doze.

"Their majesties are in the Hall of Light. I'll take you there." The man bowed then turned to a young boy waiting bright-eyed and expectant at the line of servants —a page?—and told him to tell the archivist that Del wanted to speak with her.

Then the heavy-set man led us down a long, wide hall to another grand archway, which opened into an enormous room. I wasn't certain, but I guessed most, if not all, of the city could gather within its walls.

The Hall of Light was aptly named, not because it was filled with blazing light, but because it had no roof, allowing the magical beams of rippling sunlight to fill the space, creating an airy—well watery—open feel to the space.

It only occurred to me then, that we had roofs on the surface to keep out the weather, and there wasn't any weather down here. Everything was full of water all the time, which allowed for a much different style of building. You'd still want a roof for privacy—since anyone could swim above your house—but in a hall like this, it made sense to keep it open.

The King and Queen sat at the far end of the hall on matching gleaming white thrones, but my attention was drawn to the young triton woman next to them. I guessed that was Del's sister, the princess. Long blue-black hair, just like Del's floated behind her, but her eyes, unlike Del's blue-green, were a shimmering pearl-blue. The rest of her didn't look like Del, either. Her face was slender, with a wide smile, and she gave off the impression of being delicate, almost translucent. As we drew closer, I could see it was clear that Del very much took after his father and the princess after their mother.

I glanced at Annie and was rewarded with her catching my gaze. Her cheeks lifted in what I assumed was a smile, though I couldn't see her lips to be sure. Even without a fish tail, which would allow for much greater mobility, Annie was full of grace as she swam down the length of the hall.

"The wayward son has finally returned. Shall we have a celebration?" the queen asked, her voice heavy and cutting with sarcasm. "And he's brought guests. This is new."

"Indeed it is, and a welcome change!" the king added, opening his arms in invitation. "Honored guests, welcome to our halls. Son, what brings you back to us with these surface folk?"

Del swam ahead of us to meet his parents and sister, and as he did, another triton entered. It was obvious at first glance that this was Del's younger brother. He had a mix of his parent's features, which made him delicately handsome, not rugged and large like his brother, but with the same striking blue-black hair and green-blue eyes that Del had.

"Mother. Father," Del began. I found it interesting that he addressed her first. "Luarnon. Poseia," he added, nodding to his brother and sister. "I've come here on a quick mission to do some research in the library. I've already called for Archivist Umandra, and I—"

"A quick mission?" the queen asked, cutting him off. Her eyes narrowed. "You're not staying?"

Del stiffened at the ice in her voice, and I fought back a shudder at the chill.

"No Mother, I'm not." He drew in a long breath and squared his shoulders. "And on that note, I'm renouncing my claim to the crown. I don't want it. Let Luarnon or Poseia rule in my place."

The queen's eyes flashed wide with surprise then snapped back to narrow and angry as her lips curled back in an unfriendly smile. "Of course, this is what we've come to. Running away from your responsibility permanently this time, are you?"

"I am," Del said, not even bothering to defend himself.

"Then go." She surged up out of her throne with a powerful swish of her tail, towering above everyone, her pale green hair billowing around her like a cloud. "But don't you dare return. And since you're no longer a prince, you have no right to call upon an Archivist of the Library of Galniosia!" Her smile turned into a full sneer of disgust, her face and shoulders flushing red with her fury. "I don't care why you've come. Leave now and never return!"

"No," the king roared.

Del jerked, the movement sending him back a foot, his expression shocked at his father's ferocious outburst. In fact, everyone in the hall looked stunned as if the king never raised his voice or countermanded an order from his queen.

The queen's gaze snapped to him. "I've given an order—"

"And we rule *together*. Hanea, you're my queen, my *equal*. I'm happy to let you make most of the decisions for this kingdom. When it comes to our people, you're a wise and thoughtful ruler, but not when it comes to our son. Even if Delphon wishes to give up his title, he'll always be welcome here."

"Not by me," the queen hissed. She jerked her attention back to Del, looking at him with a disgust that made me want to tell her off. It didn't matter that she was a queen. She was Del's mother. I didn't understand how she couldn't see what a strong and honorable man he was.

"I've said what I will," she snarled, then swept out of the room.

Ouch.

Yet as soon as she left, the entire feel of the room changed to one of welcome and acceptance. Del's family approached him, and he embraced each of them in turn, then they spoke quietly amongst themselves for a moment. I didn't know if they were talking about what they were going to do about the queen or not, but no one got upset and the tension from before didn't return.

"That was harsh," Annie said softly, floating up beside me, as Rion drifted closer as well.

"His mother and my father should get together," Rion said sourly. "They'd be perfect for each other."

"I apologize for my wife," the king said as Del, his father, and siblings swam toward us. The king's voice was low as if he didn't want it to carry throughout the room, which was something I could completely understand if I was the one who had to live with her. "She's... over-worked with the cares of the kingdom."

I tried to not roll my eyes. That was a polite way of putting it.

"You're abdicating?" Del's brother said, with a look of not-completely-unexpected surprise mixed with a real-ization of how overwhelming his situation now was. "I'll be king?"

"The laws state it need not be the eldest who inher-its," the princess said politely. There was a glint in her eye. I didn't think she was seeking power, but she certainly seemed more ready for it than her brother—who I presumed was older than her. She turned her attention to Del. "No offence Del, but I always assumed you'd not take the throne."

"Then perhaps you know me better than I do," he replied, not looking at all offended at her comment.

"And who are our guests?" the king asked, turning to the rest of us.

Del finally smiled. "These are my... close friends. Aethan of the Theophylian Plains, Hyperion of the Phyllidian Forest, and Annie Chambers of... Chicago," he finished awkwardly, as if he wasn't sure how to introduce Annie. And I completely understood the sentiment. How did one tell one's family that you'd fallen in love with a woman from another world and were sharing her with three other guys?

"I've not heard of this place, Chicago," the king said. "Is it far away?"

Very far, and yet not that far. I had to stop myself from laughing. It was on another world and you couldn't get there from here at all unless Annie took you. Though the rock on the shore which we travelled through was not too far from here. Again, hard to explain.

"Ah... yes," was Del's diplomatic answer.

"And what interesting coloring," the princess added, her gaze scrutinizing Annie, and I got the distinct impression—although I wasn't quite sure how, probably woman's intuition—that she already knew there was more between Del and Annie. "Dryad? *satyr*? *aurai*?"

"She's *heliai*, a Fire Titan," Rion said, saving the rest of us from having to come up with something, "and it is quite uncomfortable for her down here."

Annie nodded. "True."

The Princess' eyes widened. "Then you're from far away. Welcome to Galniosia." She gave a nod, and I got the feeling she still didn't believe us.

We were saved from further discussion by the arrival of an ancient Triton woman with silvered scales on her tail, some of which had been lost. Her hair was the same shimmering silver color, with eyes of steel-blue. There was a wiry strength in her form, denoting no lack of vigor in her old age, and my first guess was this was the Royal Archivist.

"Delphon? Finally returned and asking for me? Well that's something I thought I'd never see," she said. "You were never that interested in my studies."

"Alas, you're right, Umandra," Del said, bowing his head in apology. "And for that I'm sorry. It's because I was so lacking in my studies that I've come to you now. I seek information of the ancient gods, specifically Hera. I was hoping you'd be able to help me— *us* find out more about her."

Umandra's wispy, silvered brows rose. "Hera? In truth I'm not sure I taught you much about her. I can see why you might need to come to me."

"What's this for?" the princess asked.

"That's a long story," Del replied. "And we're in a bit of a hurry. As you can see, my friends aren't meant for the water. I'm hoping to get them back to the shore quickly." He turned to Umandra. "Is there much you can recall? Specifically, about her powers and what she could do?"

The elder Triton swayed in the water for a long moment, eyes half closed, as if falling asleep. Then she began to recite—what sounded like verbatim—text. "Hera, the reluctant bride of Zeus, and—some say—the first among the ancient gods. She held great power and import. Like Zeus she had many consorts: the healer Asclepius, Aeolus of the winds, Autolycus the thief, and even a few women, Theia and Echo." Umandra blinked, as if coming out of a trance. "There are some other vague references to binding these consorts to her and gaining their powers."

"Healing, winds, thievery, and senses?" Rion said.

Umandra shrugged. "The ancient texts and tales are never entirely correct. There may be some discrepancies, but Hera is depicted with some or all of these powers in most of them: heightened senses to spy on her husband's trysts, healing to recover from wounds quickly and rejuvenate herself, winds to bluster and blow about her enemies. Some tales tell of the few times she and Zeus worked together, she was the high winds and he the lightning of fury. As for thievery, that's more esoteric in its depictions. Often she seems to steal the very life or essence from a person. That's the least depicted of her powers. She was also known as the matron of the home, presiding over the bonding of mates, and childbirth."

That was a lot to take in. It sounded like Hera was going to be nearly impossible to defeat. Senses to see or hear us coming, healing to resist our attacks, winds to attack us with, and somehow also able to steal our very lives away?

Well... fuck.

The others didn't look that happy either.

"Why do you need this information?" Umandra asked as the entire royal family inched closer, clearly interested in the answer as well.

"Oh, no reason really," Del said, casually. "We just need to find Hera and remove her from power—probably kill her—as she's in a position of great power in another world, where she's plotting all manner of terrible things, or so we assume."

Luarnon laughed, clearly disbelieving.

It was the princess Poseia who cut him off. "By Poseidon, you're not joking, are you?" Oh, she was keen, something that would have turned me on a couple of weeks ago and now... the only woman for me was Annie.

The thought made my heart swell with joy.

"No, I'm not joking," Del said.

Luarnon stopped laughing and silence rippled through the currents around us as the shock of the situation sank in.

CHAPTER 24

ANNIE

AFTER DEL'S STUNNING REVELATION, IT HAD BEEN EASY FOR him to make apologies and say a quick goodbye to his father and siblings and for us to hurry out of the Hall of Light to return to the surface.

We swam—slowly compared to Del and the other tritons—back down the long wide hall, but when we reached the edge of the palace grounds, the princess rushed out after us.

She was alone, so whatever she suspected, she hadn't wanted to share with her father or brother.

"Del, wait. You can't be serious. What's really going on?" She swam around in front of us, and her gaze landed on me. "I know you're not *heliai*. I've never seen one, and your hair is certainly red, but that one—" She jerked her chin at Rion. "He answered too quickly and you looked worried when my father asked about your heritage. Who are you?"

I bit the inside of my cheek. I didn't know how to begin to explain that I came from another world or that

I'd bonded with Del, along with three others. That would just bring up more questions when we really needed to be coming up with a plan to stop Hera.

"We don't have time to explain," Del replied.

"Make time." A fire sparked in her pearl-blue eyes and it was clear she wasn't going to let us go without an explanation. "Are they compelling you somehow? You've never been this driven before about anything."

So that was it. She was suspicious because Del was taking action. It made my heart break a little for him. First his mother basically disowned him for refusing the crown, and now his sister was questioning him because he was actually trying to do something.

"They're not compelling me." Del frowned. "Well..."

"I knew it!" Poseia exclaimed.

I glanced at Del, uncertain why he'd hesitated. We weren't compelling him. At least I didn't think we were. I'd thought he'd wanted to bond with me. Was he having doubts?

His gaze met mine and his green-blue eyes filled with love. "I'm compelled by my heart." He turned his attention back to his sister. "I'm in love with Annie. And you're right, she isn't *heliai*. She's human. And I know that means nothing to you, but it would take too long to explain."

"She's from another world," Rion said with a shrug. "Easy to explain. Hard to understand."

"Human?" Poseia asked, but she didn't seem surprised. "There are legends of humans. They're the ones who drove us from the world of the gods."

Humans were legendary? Well that was unexpected.

Then Del's previous words must have hit home for Poseia and she frowned. "And you love her?"

Her frown deepened as if she couldn't understand what seemed so simple to me and probably everyone else, and her gaze swept over me. "You don't have a body made for water, but... you're not without strengths. Attractive... in an exotic and foreign way."

I snorted. Those words had never been said about me by anyone, ever, until now. But I guess from her perspective, I was exotic and foreign.

"Thank you," I said, not sure what else I should say.

The princess turned back to Del and examined him. "You two truly are bound by something, aren't you?"

Del met her gaze head on, waiting for her to come to the realization that he hadn't lied about us being in love.

"You really are in love. You've bonded with her!" Her surprise blossomed into a brilliant smile. "By the gods, Del, I never thought you'd find *the* woman for you." Her gaze jumped to Rion and Aethan and she cocked an eyebrow. "And these others, the way they look at you and her— Oh!"

A mix of emotions flashed through her expression and I bit my tongue, watching her realize the truth, afraid of what her reaction would be.

"You're *all* in love with her." She nodded, her expression settling on understanding and... I wasn't quite sure. Was that pride?

"You've changed brother. Matured. You were never one for settling down, nor for sharing, but you've never looked more content." Her smile faded. "So, what's this talk of fighting Hera? A dead goddess? It makes no sense."

Del opened his mouth, closed it, then opened it and closed it again as if he couldn't figure out how to respond to his sister.

"Your highness," Aethan said to the princess. "If you can accept the strangeness of Annie's heritage and our... relationships with each other, perhaps there is another strangeness, a mystery you can accept as well. The world of the gods you mentioned isn't legend, it's real. But not many can travel between that world and ours. Annie is one who can. Hera is another. She lives in this other world and doesn't use her god-like abilities for the good of all people. She needs to be stopped."

The princess nodded, her gaze turning inward as if in thought. "If only a select few can pass from one world to the other, that would explain why it's been lost to us for thousands of years. You're a group full of many wonders, not the least of which is my brother bonding with such strange folk and dedicating himself to a woman from another world." She swam over to Del, grasped his shoulders and looked deep into his sea-green eyes. "If you survive what's to come, we'll need to have a long talk."

He nodded. "Indeed."

She released him. "Father and Luarnon will have questions, but I'll make explanations for you," she said, motioning to the seaweed forest at the edge of the city. "Go."

"She's very perceptive," Rion said softly as we swam away.

"No kidding." I glanced back, but she was already swimming back to the palace.

"It was always hard to slip anything past her, even as a child," Del said. "And she's grown up a lot since then." He sounded a bit wistful. "Perhaps more than I have, even though she's the youngest."

"Facing off against your mother, renouncing your throne. I think you've grown up well," I said softly.

He smiled at me, glided over, and brushed his lips against my cheek. Then he led us onward to shore. We didn't return to Masia, but to the beach near the black rocks where we could travel between worlds. The boat with Keph would have travelled much faster than we had, and as expected, Keph was already at the stones waiting for us.

Once on dry land, after some struggling, we managed to get the huphelopoid off our faces. The three of us who'd worn them all took deep breaths of the fresh sea air, happy to be done with the stinky things. Then we told Keph everything we'd learned. He, like the rest of us, wasn't happy about the situation.

Now, after having discussed our options, we stood before the rocks, working up the nerve to go.

I looked at each one of my guys, making sure our eyes connected so I could show them with a look how much I loved them while trying not to show how much I was afraid I'd lose them.

"Are we ready for this?" I asked, tugging on my winter clothes.

We'd all gotten dressed again, ready for winter in

Chicago, but after being comfortably naked for over a day, the clothes didn't feel right any more.

"I suspect Hera was listening to us through our phones, but just in case, we need to be ready for her as soon as we get through to the other side," I said.

The guys nodded, their expressions hard with determination.

The plan was simple, but I needed to go over it again to reassure myself. From Keph's vision, we already knew Hera was at the top of a building down town. We just needed to get there and hopefully surprise her.

"Aethan and Rion will flag down a cab, preferably two. Del, Keph, and I will head to a bar I know and use their phone to call my FBI friend. Hopefully Hera won't have every phone tapped. We'll need Janice's help for the next part. Then we meet up, get in the cabs, and off we go. Ready?"

Nods all around.

This was it.

I touched the stone, and we all stepped through returning to Chicago and to a fight I was less and less certain we could win.

CHAPTER 25

KEPHAS

THE ROAR OF THE *HELICOPTER*, AS ANNIE CALLED IT, WAS intense even through the ear-muffling headgear we wore.

I'd never thought to experience flying. I was far too heavy to be lifted by Rion or any other winged race back home, yet in this world, there were machines that could lift many people. Funny enough, out of all of us, Del wasn't handling the flight well, his expression pinched and his complexion green. I, on the other hand, was loving it.

Annie had called her friend at the— *what is the name? Oh, right*— the FBI and arranged the flight, and now the city was flashing by below us.

My vision from before we'd left Annie's world had told me Hera lived at the top of a tall building at the center of the city, near the lake—the vision had even given me the name of the building.

But the building had presented us with a problem: how to get all of us past a building full of people to get to that top floor.

The solution was this flying craft. We'd be dropped off on the roof, right above Hera, although with the din of the machine, I suspected we'd lose any sense of surprise. Hopefully, however, that would be balanced out by our quick arrival on scene. And while Hera could call for help, if they were coming from elsewhere in the building, they'd need a little time to get there. With luck, we'd be in and out before that help could arrive.

It was a daring plan, but I believed in Annie and the rest of the guys. We could do this. Well, we could get in and out, but whether we could deal with Hera... that remained to be seen.

Del tapped my arm and pointed at the large building we were rapidly approaching. This was it. There was a large flat spot at the top of the building, though it didn't have an "H" like the place where we'd first gotten into the *helicopter*.

The craft swooped in and touched down deftly. The plan was that it would only wait for us for a few minutes, so we threw open the door and rushed out, determined to deal with Hera as quickly as possible.

Aethan was the first to the door. "I'll go scout things out as you all get down there!" he shouted over the roar of the *helicopter*, then he was off like a blur.

I got out next. Being the biggest and hardest to hurt, I was to act like a wall and protect them in case we were met right away with an attack.

No one came to stop us and we hurried to the narrow stairs—almost too narrow for me—and headed down to Hera's floor. Del followed behind me then Rion and finally Annie accompanied by the FBI woman, Janice.

We reached the first floor down, and met up with Aethan who was waiting for us in the stairwell.

"This place is huge," he said. "Her living quarters are two levels and it looks like we're in a private stairwell. There are guards outside Hera's main door, but I locked it on them and I hope they don't have a key. That should give us some time."

"Good," Annie said.

"I also think Hera is in there alone," Aethan added. "Which is a great stroke of luck!"

"That remains to be seen," Del said behind me, echoing my own thoughts.

"This way." Aethan led us out of the stairwell into an opulent hall with bright lights and a marble floor to a set of double doors.

"I think she's in here," Aethan whispered. "I caught sight of her from a balcony outside during my scouting."

"Indeed I am," Hera called from inside. "Come on in, Annie."

I huffed a heavy breath. We hadn't expected surprise, but it would have been nice.

Aethan pulled open the door, revealing a large room. It was lavishly decorated with thick carpets and many tables and cushioned chairs. Along the far wall stood a bank of floor-to-ceiling windows looking out over a large, sprawling balcony, and beyond that the lake.

Hera wore a silk wrap tied tight about her waist, accentuating her thin figure. It was colorful with flowers and birds depicted on it. She tossed her black hair back with a casual hand and peered at me, hungrily, as if she wanted to eat me, making my chest tighten with fear. The look was unnerving and she didn't seem worried about us at all. Something I didn't like.

And yet she seemed so small and defenseless. Maybe I could just grab her and be done with this.

I started forward and reached to grab her, but she seized one of my outstretched hands and I felt— I couldn't quite describe it. It was as if lightning shot through my entire being. Then the world was spinning and she casually tossed me across the room.

Annie called out my name and I landed hard, my breath knocked out of me.

"This was a mistake, Annie," Hera sneered. "You can't hope to win against me, and I can't be killed, so what was your plan?"

Aethan ran forward too fast for me to see. I was guessing he tried to grab her as well, but she blurred, as if she was moving as fast as he was, and he was flying through the air and crashing into a table beside me with a heavy grunt of pain.

"Unless, of course, you've come to hand over your men to me?" Hera purred. "That's very kind of you."

Annie's face had gone pale, the speckles on her cheeks dark in contrast, and her eyes were wide with fear.

I climbed to my feet as Rion and Del fanned out, looking at Hera warily, not sure what to do, while the FBI woman had her weapon out and pointed at Hera.

"June Olympios," Janice said, "come willingly and you won't be hurt."

Hera threw her head back and laughed. "Oh, Annie. You brought a poor civilian into this, too?" With a casual flick of her fingers, a wind gust swept through the room, knocking over a few chairs, and slammed into Janice. The woman flew back, crashing out the doors and tumbling into the hall.

"I don't know—" Hera groaned and dropped to one knee as her gaze jerked to Del and locked on him. "This is new. I haven't been attacked by a water-bearer in a while."

Grimacing, she slowly rose. Her body trembled, but her gaze never left Del, who was now also trembling and starting to curl in on himself.

His complexion started to turn gray and horrible realization hit me. "She's stealing our powers!"

It made sense. She'd thrown me like she had the same strength as me. Then she'd moved as quickly as Aethan, and was now using Del's powers against him.

"So that's what thievery meant," Aethan mumbled. "Well, fuck! How do we fight someone who has all of our powers plus her own?"

"Exactly," Hera sneered, her voice cold and deadly. She straightened and clenched her fist. Del screamed and collapsed, writhing on the floor in agony. "You don't have a chance against me. Give up now and I'll let you all live long enough to have a nice, sappy goodbye. Persist, and I'll kill you all in an instant."

A loud bang rang out and Hera screamed as blood sprayed out of her neck. She choked and clamped a hand over the wound, gasping for air, her eyes wide and stunned.

I rushed in, hoping the wound would disable her enough for me to knock her out. I swung a backhand at her temple with all my strength, and she caught it without even grunting with effort.

She glared at me with her silver-blue eyes and a feral smile, as the wound on her neck bled less and less, and closed up.

Then she squeezed and for the first time in a long time, I felt pain as her fingers dug into my hand. She seemed able to bypass my greater durability, nails digging in and drawing blood.

"This is your choice?" she hissed. "Big mistake."

She kicked between my legs and I nearly blacked out with pain and shock. I flew across the room, crashing through the furniture, but didn't really notice. That didn't hurt as much as her kick had.

The guys yelled and screamed, cries of pain and dismay filled the room, but my world was spinning on the edge of unconsciousness at the agony. I couldn't see, let alone stand up and fight, and I could only pray the others could succeed where I couldn't.

CHAPTER 26

ANNIE

NOTHING WAS WORKING AND EVERYTHING WAS GOING wrong. I needed to do something and quick. I'd been stunned and uncertain so far, watching my guys get tossed about the room and tormented, but it had to stop.

Except what could I do? Hera had access to all my powers plus her own.

Rion was the only one of the guys still standing, since he hadn't acted yet. We glanced at each other and nodded, and I prayed he'd had the same idea I had.

I launched myself at Hera with Aethan's speed and closed my eyes, as Rion—on cue—blinded her with a flash of light.

Please work. Please, God.

The flashed dissipated, and I opened my eyes again to see Hera in front of me, stunned, blinking.

Good.

I hit her hard, tackling her to the ground. I didn't really know how to fight, but I hoped a super-strength slap, might just do her in. I reared back, sitting on her, and sent my hand flying, but she somehow caught it, even with her eyes closed.

"Bad girl!" she growled.

With a vise-like grip, she crushed my wrist, my bones shattering. Agony tore through me, drawing a scream as tears streamed down my cheeks.

A gust of wind slammed me into the ceiling, stealing my breath and making the world lurch, and I crashed back to the hard floor face-first, a dozen feet away from her. Pain sliced through my face and blood rushed from my nose.

Rion screamed, and he charged toward Hera, but she punched him with bone-crushing strength fueled by Keph's power. His ribs broke with a resounding *crack* and he flew across the room, slammed into the wall, and sagged to the floor, unconscious.

God, no!

My soul screamed. I was going to lose him. I was going to lose all of them.

I reached out to him with my healing powers. His pulse stuttered then stopped and my pulse lurched in fear as I flooded him with my magic. She'd almost killed him. If I'd been a second later, he would have died.

I pushed everything I could into Rion and watched his body convulse with the sudden healing. Strength returned to him, as it ebbed out of me. He was alive, but didn't regain consciousness.

I healed myself next, but only used enough power so my wounds wouldn't distract me, knitting my wrist back together so I could use my hand and easing the pain in my face. I didn't have a lot of power left after saving Rion and I couldn't afford to pass out from exhaustion. Not yet anyway.

Three more shots in quick succession roared through the room and Hera screamed again.

I forced myself to sit up as Janice hurried to my side and knelt next to me.

"You okay?"

"I'll be fine." But even as I said that, Hera rose from where she'd fallen, three bloody gunshot holes in her silk kimono showing her healing flesh beneath.

Del's Royal Archivist had said Hera could heal—so it didn't matter if she was using my power or not—but the gunshots were still knocking her down and forcing her to expend power. And if I had a limit, she had to have one, too.

"Keep firing at her!" I told Janice. So far that was the only thing that seemed to work.

We rose together and Janice fired three more shots. The first clipped a shoulder as Hera moved, zipping like Aethan, suddenly disappearing and reappearing right beside us.

"You've been a naughty girl, Annie. For that, you'll pay the dearest price!"

She grabbed the gun from Janice's hands and shoved the woman away. Janice tumbled across the floor, bumping to a stop at the windows overlooking the balcony.

"For your insolence, I'm going to take what you prize most," Hera sneered with the tigress grin, and she slapped a heavy hand over my heart.

I tried to jerk away, but something in her touch seized

my muscles, freezing me in place, making it impossible for me to move. Then agony tore into me and I felt my life being ripped out.

I screamed, as her power sliced deep, reaching past my body, my cells, and tearing into my soul. Everything I was rushed out of me, and time stuttered into horrific slow motion, the horror and agony being drawn out while my mind and body howled.

Then she stepped back, and I sagged to my knees, gasping and empty... and not dead.

I didn't understand how I was still alive, how she could take everything from me and I was still—

My pulse stalled.

I couldn't feel their powers.

I couldn't feel *them*.

My connection with my guys was gone.

My bonds were gone!

Please. No.

I mentally clawed inside me, desperate to find our connection, desperate to rebuild the connection with them. But I was empty. Completely hollowed out, as if my heart and soul had been removed and I was now just a shell—

Except I wasn't empty. There was something deep within me, something small and strange, and it connected me to... Hera.

Oh, God.

Hera's eyes widened as if she, too, had just figured out we were connected, but her shock twisted into evil satisfaction and she shoved me back.

I stumbled and fell onto my butt. The impact jarred

up my spine, but the pain was nothing compared to the empty agony of losing my bonds.

Hera laughed. "You were a fool to go up against the goddess of bonds, Annie. Who do you think made such things even possible? It was me! That is my ultimate power. To make and break bonds, and I've just taken yours."

"No." *Please no.* Except I knew the truth. I could *feel* it.

Her laugh rose to a crescendo. "What a wonderful look on your face. Such beautiful horror. I'd savor it, but I'm not that dumb. It's time for you to die."

She slapped her hands together and a blast of wind slammed into me, throwing me back and crashing me through the windows. Glass tore through my clothes and sliced into my back as I flew over the balcony. The backs of my legs hit the glass half-wall at the edge of the balcony, breaking bones—as well as the glass, which sliced into my calves—and sent me tumbling backwards around and around.

For a second, I was suspended in the air, time once again slowing as I realized Janice had been caught up in the blast as well, thrown out over the edge like me.

Then time lurched back to normal and I fell. The world spun around and around, sky, ground, buildings, the wind from my fall stinging my skin.

I tried to control my water, make myself float like I had when I'd made love with Rion—

But I no longer had Del's powers.

Oh, God. They're gone.

And Rion was still unconscious and couldn't release his wings and rescue me.

There was nothing and no one who could help me.

Nothing.

Nothing but the ground rushing up to meet me.

To be continued...

in the third and final book in The Grecian Goddess

Trilogy – Bonds of the Goddess.

Don't miss the final book in the series!

BONDS OF THE GODDESS
Grecian Goddess Trilogy: Book 3

She's a lover, not a fighter. But threaten her guys, and she'll fight like hell...

When you're in the fight of your life, it's best not to underestimate your opponent. Which is exactly how Annie Chambers finds herself plummeting from the top of a highrise, easily flicked out the window by Hera.

Things go downhill from there. Only she and Delphon escape Hera's clutches. Rion, Keph, and Aethan remain trapped. And that's not the most desperate thing about the situation.

Hera has ripped away Annie's soul bonds with all four of her guys, leaving her empty, heartbroken, defeated. No matter how hard she and Del try—and gods, do they try—there's no way to restore the bond. Without the love, passion, and power flowing from her guys, what does she have left?

They need help, and the only place to find it is in the other world. But even if Annie and Del can gather an army, the horrible truth remains. They might win the war, but Annie's soul bonds with her guys could be lost forever.

OTHER BOOKS BY TESSA COLE

THE NEPHILIM'S DESTINY SERIES

Destined Shadows, prequel story

Destined Darkness, book 1

Destined Blood, book 2

Destined Fire, book 3

Destined Storm, book 4

Destined Radiance, book 5

THE ANGEL'S FATE SERIES

Fated Bonds, book 1

Fated Winter, book 2

Fated Fear, book 3

Fated Despair, book 4

Fated Resolve, book 5

Fated Heart, book 6

THE GRECIAN GODDESS TRILOGY

Kiss of the Goddess, book 1

Power of the Goddess, book 2

Bonds of the Goddess, book 3

OTHER BOOKS BY CLARA WILS

THE GRECIAN GODDESS TRILOGY

Kiss of the Goddess, book 1

Power of the Goddess, book 2

Bonds of the Goddess, book 3